RIVER CITY
INFERNO

RIVER CITY
INFERNO
A Colonial Mystery

By
Peter Newman Tarbutton

My gratitude and thanks to Germain J. Bienvenu, Ph.D., Special Collections Public Services, Louisiana State University Libraries, Baton Rouge, LA, for his invaluable assistance in the production of copies of historical records from the Papeles Procedentes de Cuba, Cuban Papers and the Audiencia de Santo Domingo, Santo Domingo Papers Collections.

I also wish to thank the Honorable Dale N. Adkins, Clerk of Civil District Court, Parish of Orleans, and Siva Blake, Deputy Clerk, for their outstanding assistance in the preparation of copies of Notarial Acts from the Notarial Archives Research Center, New Orleans, LA.

Chapter 1

The trip up the Mississippi River to New Orleans took about twelve hours as Captain Angus had predicted. The breeze would rise, pick up the sails and move the ship, then die down again, and repeat. It was monotonous. He became very bored and turned in at sunset. Just before he fell asleep, he thought about how he had not compromised his cover story during the long journey from Cadiz, Spain.

The weather here was different compared to the Atlantic coast of Spain six weeks earlier. There had been a cool breeze and warm sunshine after they entered the Gulf of Mexico a week ago. He looked forward to living in a pleasant climate such as this.

He recalled what the booking agent told him before he bought the ticket.

"The name of the ship is the *Adriana* and she has made the voyage many times before. You need not worry, it will only take about four weeks at the most."

That was a lie. There were many storms and the sea was always rough. The trip required more than six weeks to arrive at this point.

The only good thing about the trip was the friendship that developed between he and Captain Angus. During the storms, they spent many hours below deck playing cards and enjoying glasses of Madeira.

When he awoke the next morning, the ship had already landed at New Orleans. It was on the quay, a strip of land along the river's edge where boats usually unloaded. Here there were no wooden docks as he had seen in Liverpool, England or Cadiz.

Standing on the deck he looked around at the surroundings and began to think about how much he was looking forward to this assignment. A spy for the British army. He recalled what Major Pullman said two months ago during his final briefing in Newgate Prison in London.

"Now here is the plan. We have prepared for you false Spanish identity papers. They will say that you are a medically discharged Spanish soldier who was wounded in the line of duty. Just in case someone challenges that, you will use that scar on your back as proof. Occasionally fake a limp when the weather is bad. Here is £200. It is for you to buy some decent clothes. Make sure you get a pair of riding boots.

"Here are some additional papers. One is your permit to travel in England. You will need it as you move about in London getting yourself outfitted.

"Next, make your way to Liverpool and book passage on a ship bound for Lisbon, Portugal. Stay there a fortnight. Say that you are recuperating from fever as a cover story. Finally, you will book passage to Cadiz, Spain, and on to New Orleans. That will be your destination.

"Your cover story there will be that you are searching for a plantation in the Colony close to the city. When, you find one, the money to buy it will be advanced to you.

"As I said before, your job will be to collect information on the Spanish military, especially its movements. From time to time, another undercover agent will contact you to retrieve that information. Do not try to find him, he will locate you," the major explained.

He ended his speech with a frown on his face saying, "Good luck ol' chap."

Then he paused for a few seconds and looked at him firmly and said, "And try not to muck it up!"

After breakfast, he disembarked and looked around for someone to carry his trunk and bags. When he looked to his left he could see the two ships that had preceded them up the river the night before. One was the schooner *Governor Miro*. He remembered what Angus had explained to him the day before. That ship would transport slaves, and the conditions on board were atrocious. One hundred twenty slaves would be chained together below deck, laying side by side on their backs. They were given little food or water and were not allowed to stand upright. When the sea became rough they wanted to vomit onto each other. He remembered how uncomfortable he felt when Angus told him about the slaves.

There on the quay, lined up along the river, were several men with horse-drawn carts of all sizes. Some of the carts were already loaded with baggage from the other ships there. Since there was no wooden dock, the passengers and crew had to walk down a narrow board, the gang-plank, to the shore line. The men whose carts were empty had gathered about the gang-plank of the *Adriana*. As he stepped down onto the plank one of the crew helped him with his bags.

"Are these men and their carts very reliable?" he asked.

"Oh yes, sir," the crewman responded. "These carts may look old, but they are strong enough."

"How about the drivers, do you recommend anyone in particular?"

Pointing to the driver on the right side of the plank the crewman said, "I would go with him sir."

"Good," he said.

As the crewman was helping the driver load the cart he asked the driver, "How much to take me to a room for rent?"

The driver said, "My name is Pedro and it will be one gold centavo."

He immediately turned to the crewman with a questioning look on his face.

The crewman shrugged his shoulders, nodded and said in a strong Spanish accent, "It is fair."

Pedro put out his hand as though he was expecting him to put the coin in it.

"Pedro, my name is Santiago de Barcelona," he said with a stern look on his face. "And I will pay you after you have put my baggage in my room."

"Oh, yes, sir," Pedro said, with a very big grin on his face. "Now, sir, if you will step up on to de cart we will be ready to go."

Off to his left Santiago noticed a commotion of some sort with much yelling, by several men. They were close to the ship *Governor Miro*. Without warning a slave, wearing only trousers and no shoes, broke away from several Pardo guards. He had somehow managed to get his hands on one of the guard's bayonet.

He was running very fast straight toward Santiago with the bayonet in his right hand high in the air. All the while, he was yelling something that Santiago could not understand and he could see his eyes were wide open with the look of terror. Suddenly he heard the loud sound of a shot from a musket. The ball struck the man in the back of the head, taking off the top of it. Blood splattered everywhere around as well as all over Santiago's face and clothes. His new white shirt, that he was wearing for the first time, had little red dots all over it.

"OH MY GOD!" he cried out loudly. He turned and looked down at the man lying face up on the ground in front of him. The man's eyelids were only partly open now. His eyeballs were rolled half way up into what was left of his head.

The guard came running up and stood over the dead man. He then bent over, picked up his bayonet and very calmly replaced it into its sheath.

At that point Santiago turned around so as not to look at the dead man. There, under the cart, was Pedro face down in the dirt with his hands covering the back of his head. He reached down and helped Pedro out.

"Are you all right?" Santiago asked.

"Yes," Pedro exclaimed with a shaky voice.

"If you are going to carry this thing you had better learn how to use it! Santiago exclaimed, handing Pedro's pistol back to him.

"Thank you, sir," Pedro said, still shaking.

"Let's get out of here before the crowd gathers," Santiago said, afraid the incident may draw attention to him.

He climbed onto the cart. While sitting there he saw Pedro walk over to the crewman and say something in a low voice. The crewman nodded and Pedro walked to the cart. He wondered what Pedro said to the crewman.

As the cart pulled away toward the dirt road, it made a rocking motion back and forth with the baggage sliding one way and then back. Santiago quickly grabbed the side of the seat. There was only one seat and both he and Pedro sat on it together.

The road was very bumpy with many ruts and pot holes. The cart bounced along.

He asked Pedro, "Are all the roads like this one?"

Pedro answered with a smile, "Oh no, sir, many worse."

"Maybe we will get to where I am going before my spine gets driven into my skull," he said, in a nervous tone.

Finally, they came to a smooth stretch in the road. The horse slowed a little as pulling the cart was easier now.

"Does that sort of thing with the slaves happen often?" Santiago asked.

"No, only once in a while," he replied. "Dat Pardo will probably get two silver pesos for stopping dat slave."

As they traveled a little further, Santiago turned and looked back. There was a crowd of people now gathered around where they had been. He thought it was a good idea that they left the scene immediately, and not be seen there by the authorities.

"Do you know a gentleman by the name of Diego de Castellano?" Pedro asked, breaking the momentary silence.

"No, who is this de Castellano fellow?" Santiago asked.

"He is a man who buys and sells things," Pedro answered.

"Such as?" Santiago asked, in a demanding tone.

"Oh slaves, or horses, or pelts and furs he gets from da trappers who come down da river. Sometimes houses, such as the one I am taking you to," Pedro said. "Not much goes on here dat Señor Diego do not know about."

"Did he happen to say where I might eat my supper tonight?" Santiago asked.

Pedro said, "Dat is an easy one. See dat bistro on de right we just went by? De one with tables out front? It be a good place. I know de manager. Free woman of color, she is, named Roseta Robin. Never be disappointed dere. And dat is Señor Diego's favorite night place."

Santiago began to wonder. *Is this Diego his contact. Is Pedro a part of the ring? And what about the crewman from the ship? Are they also involved?*

It did seem strange that this Pedro fellow knew so much about his arrival. He felt uneasy about the possibility of his cover being compromised, but decided to worry about that later. All he wanted to do at that moment was to get settled into a nice cozy room with a soft bed.

Chapter 2

As they turned onto Saint Pierre Street, Pedro pointed out the homes of the government officials on the left across the street from the Plaza de Armas.

"Dese are the finest homes in da city," he explained.

Santiago, questioning his truthfulness, asked, "And tell me, my friend, just how do you know these things? Have you been inside all of them?"

"Most dem," he answered. "You see I's do small jobs for dem from time to time."

"And when you do these jobs, do you get to see the young ladies who work there?"

Pedro hesitated for a few seconds before answering then smiled and said, "It is possible."

"Oh, I think it is more like probably," Santiago said quickly.

Pedro did not answer, but gave out a hearty laugh.

By now, they were one block on Saint Pierre and Pedro pointed out the church and the housing for the priests on the right.

"Do you know Tomas the priest?" Santiago asked.

"He is my cousin and I have not seen him for many years. Is that where he lives?"

"Yes," Pedro answered.

Then, the cart began to slow down considerably. The wheels were beginning to sink down deeply into the very wet mud and horse manure. Santiago looked over the edge of the cart, he could see the wheel on that side was down in the muck up to the axle. As he looked further down the street in front, he could see that this awful smelly muck extended several blocks.

"Is the mud always this bad?" Santiago asked.

"No, sometimes after de rain, it worse," Pedro answered.

"I cannot imagine anything worse than this."

Pedro explained, "In da late summer when da big blow comes, da river floods da city. Afterwards, dead fish everywhere, and da smell, much worse dan dis."

"I suppose we have no other choice."

"I am afraid not," Pedro answered in an apologetic tone.

"I tell you the quicker we get out of this the better I will feel," Santiago stated, holding a handkerchief over his nose

Pedro handed the reins to Santiago and said, "You take dese and guide da horse, I get out and push."

In about one-half minute, from behind the cart came the words, "Okay make de horse go."

Santiago popped the reins on the horse's rump and she began to move. Then the cart suddenly lurched ahead. Pedro quickly ran alongside the moving cart and jumped up onto the seat. Santiago quickly handed him the reins. He looked down at the knee-high riding boots that Pedro was wearing. They were caked with the muck almost to the top. The pungent odor, that was previously down on the street, was now up in the cart next to him.

Pedro saw what he was looking at and laughingly said, "De boots, dey come in handy, no?"

Santiago, holding his hand over his nose and mouth, said nothing. Instead, he only nodded.

Continuing on Saint Pierre, the street began to smooth a little and the muck was not so deep. The odor was still there, but the horse was now having less trouble pulling the cart.

Pedro, while pointing off into the distance to the left said, "As we cross da Bourbon Street you can see da houses for the soldiers about a block over dere."

"So, do all the soldiers live there?" Santiago asked.

"No," Pedro answered. "One building is for soldiers, other for powder and guns."

"Do you mean big guns?"

Pedro shook his head and said, "Just muskets."

Santiago, thinking this would be a good time to get information from him on how much he knew about them, asked, "Do you know the name of the regiment?"

"I dink it da Louisiana Regiment," he answered.

"How about the commanding officer?"

"Uh, I dink it Pardee? Oh no, it Pardon, first name like me, Pedro."

He said excitedly, "I know this thing; I run errands for dem all da time."

"You mean you run these errands every day?"

"Well, bout. Da coronel and da other officers."

"Do they pay you?"

"Oh si, but best just after payday."

"Does the coronel pay better than the capitánes?"

"Most times, but not always," Pedro answered. "When de capitánes have dance or dinner party with their women, I get more to help."

Santiago thought to himself, *that Pedro, with his knowledge of the citizens here, especially the soldiers, could be a great source of information to him in the future.*

Chapter 3

As they approached the next corner, Santiago felt it would be a good time to change the subject.

"When will we get to the boarding house?" Santiago asked.

They began to slow as they turned the corner onto Dauphine Street.

Pedro said, "Here it is, Señor Santiago. Dis de widow Tourneur's house. She has it for rent."

Santiago stepped out of the cart in front of the two story house.

He turned toward the cart and said, "I thought you understood that all I wanted was a large room. Not the whole house."

He said nervously, "A large house such as this would be very expensive, not to mention it is much more than I need."

"Oh but, Señor," was all that Pedro could get out of his mouth before Santiago interrupted him.

"I would need at least two, maybe three servants, just to take care of this place!"

"Dis was dat Señor Diego's doing," Pedro said sheepishly. "Was all done up by him and da widow."

Santiago paused for a moment without speaking.

"I am sorry, I should not have yelled at you," he said humbly. "You are right in what you are doing," he said. "Even though it is a large house I am sure it will do just fine. It has been a long trip and I am very tired. I do not feel like looking at any other places now. So bring in the baggage and I can get unpacked and maybe rest for awhile."

As Pedro was struggling to get the trunk through the front door, Santiago, standing close by, muttered under his breath, "I am beginning to wonder about this guy Diego."

"What you say?" Pedro asked.

"Oh never mind, here I will help you," he said and they both moved the trunk up the stairs.

"Here, before I forget," he said.

Then, he thrust the one gold centavo into Pedro's hand.

He thought to himself, *it may have been too much, but that will probably secure him to me as a source of information.*

After they finished unloading the cart, Pedro climbed aboard and took the reins.

"Thank you for all your help and tell this fellow Diego that I am very much interested in meeting him," Santiago said.

"I do dat," Pedro answered as he turned the horse on to the road.

Santiago went inside and closing the door behind him, went up the stairs to the large bedroom on the second floor. In that room were the trunk and the bags. He opened each and began to sort them out. After going over to the armoire to hang up his coats, he sat on the side of the bed. For a moment, he reminisced about his long journey. How nice it had been to make a friend like Angus. Then, he noticed how soft and comfortable the bed was. He completely forgot about going to Olivier's restaurant. The sitting position became a lying position and soon he was fast asleep.

Chapter 4

He awoke to the odor of coffee and bacon frying and the sound of someone cooking in the kitchen. The kitchen was a little house just outside, adjacent to the dining area of the main house. The windows of the second story bedroom were open as were the ones downstairs. The weather was very pleasant for first day of March 1788, with a light breeze off of the river.

He quickly dressed and headed down stairs, however, he found no one in the house. He entered into the kitchen, and there was an older woman at the stove with her back towards him. She was tall, with a slender build and wearing a full length dress. Her slightly graying red hair was tied back with a white scarf. He thought this must be the widow Tourneur. Gently knocking on the door, he stepped inside.

"Hello, my name is Santiago, and you must be Mrs. Tourneur."

"Why yes," she said with a French accent. She turned toward him holding a hot skillet full of bacon.

"I hope you did not mind me approaching you this way since we had not been formally introduced," he explained, in a humble tone.

"Oh that is a nice thought, but as you will find here in this city, we are not so formal," she said, after putting the skillet on the side burner to cool. While they talked he stayed by the door and she across the room by the stove.

"The breakfast will be ready shortly. You can go into the dining room and sit at the table. I'll be there momentarily with the food."

He did as he was told, and did not know what to think about all of this pleasant hospitality. Surely, she was not planning to be the cook.

After he walked into the dining area, he noticed a painting of an older man hanging on the wall. He assumed that was her deceased husband.

The table was made of oak with thick legs and a polished surface. There were four chairs to match. As he was looking at the painting, she came in behind him.

"That is my late husband," she said. "He has been gone about five years now."

"He is a very distinguished looking gentleman, was he in the military?" Santiago asked.

"Yes, for many years," she replied.

"That is something to be very proud of," he said.

"Thank you," she answered, as she placed the plates of hot rolls, bacon and a mug of coffee in front of him.

It was at that point that he noticed there was only one place set at the table.

"This is most kind of you, ma'am, but aren't you going to eat also?"

"Oh I have already eaten, you see it is almost ten o'clock in the morning and I have been up since the rooster crowed."

Santiago, felt embarrassed and did not know quite what to say.

She explained, "Now, the house rents for eight pesos, Mexican silver, per month. It will be up to you to hire your own servants to take care of the place. The rent is due on the first of each month. This first month's rent has already been taken care of. So you may pay beginning next month."

"Tell me, who paid this first month's rent?" he asked.

"Your friend, Diego," the widow replied.

"This hospitality is absolutely wonderful, not to mention that the food is very tasty. Why this unexpected pleasure?" Santiago asked.

"You see," she began. "Your cousin Tomas was very kind to us, that is my sons and I, when my husband died. He never allowed us to repay him for his kindness. So I felt like this was the least I could do."

"How did you know I was his cousin?" he asked with a smile.

"He told us about you a few years ago. I must go now. I live with my cousin, also a widow, over on Urseline Street. You can find me there when you come to pay the rent."

"Yes, of course," he said as she walked out the door.

After eating, he sat there at the table. He looked around the room, and at the picture, thinking he had never felt this welcome before. It was a wonderful feeling. It was great to know a perfect stranger had gone out of their way for him, yet asked nothing in return.

That afternoon he made he walked on Saint Pierre Street three blocks to the church. The going was slow with careful steps to avoid the mud and horse manure. As he approached the church, he saw several priests in the yard behind the building. They appeared to be discussing something in the flower garden. As he drew closer, he could see one of them that looked like Tomas. He walked over to where they were standing.

"Hello cousin Tomas!" he shouted from ten feet away.

Tomas looked up with surprise and said, "Oh hello there," and he looked at Santiago with a curious stare.

"It is me, your cousin Santiago de Barcelona."

"Oh my goodness it is you," Tomas began. "I almost did not recognize you. It has been so long. The last time we were together, you were only about fourteen years old. And look at you now, a handsome young man."

"I could recognize you anywhere cousin," Santiago said with a smile.

"You were always the flattering one," Tomas said.

"Am I interrupting you? If so I can come back at another time?" Santiago asked.

"Oh, no, no, my son. We were only admiring the flowers. Come, let us sit on the bench. Then you can tell me about your trip and why you are here."

While on their way over to the garden bench, Tomas introduced Santiago to three other priests who were just leaving. When they were alone Santiago told him all about his trip and the voyage from Cadiz and how he made friends with the ship's capitán. He also told him about Pedro, and the house he rented.

Although they talked for a long time, he was very careful not to mention his real reason for being there. After a couple of hours, Santiago began to feel like he was overstaying his welcome. So, he said goodbye, for now, and promised to meet with him again as soon as he could.

Chapter 5

He could not believe how nice a person the widow was and wondered if other people in this city would be so kind.

He remembered that he had not put his room in order since he arrived. He quickly went up the stairs. The good breakfast and the widow's kindness had given him a burst of energy.

While sorting out his clothes, he heard a voice calling from outside in the front of the house. He could hear the voice, but he could not make out the words. He walked into the other room across the hall, which had a window facing the street. When he looked out, he saw Pedro sitting on his cart in the road, just in front of the door.

"Pedro, how are you doing this fine morning?" he asked.

"I am fine, Señor Santiago. I have brought you a horse and saddle to look at. Try it out to see if you like it."

Tied to the back of Pedro's cart was a fine looking chestnut mare. On the horse's back was a new saddle with a shiny silver horn.

"I will put on my riding boots and be right down."

"Whose horse is this?" Santiago asked, as he walked through the front door.

"If you like, you can buy her and de saddle from Señor Andres Burns," Pedro answered. "Señor Diego told me to bring her dis morning. He said for me to tell you not to worry about de deal, dat he would help you take care of it."

By now, Santiago was becoming used to Diego's kindly gestures. He remembered the old saying *never look a gift horse in the mouth*, but he just had to ask.

"How old do you think she is?"

"Oh, I's knows she is a little over three years. I seen her when she was a colt."

"She is a fine looking animal," Santiago said, as he gently rubbed his hand under her belly and then over her rump. Next, he looked at the hoofs.

"I think she is in fine shape. Has she been well fed?" Santiago asked.

"Oh yes, she was kept at Burns's pasture down da street at de corner. Dere de horses always gets plenty water 'n oats," Pedro answered.

"I will ride her in a few minutes, but first I have a small chore to finish," Santiago said. He untied her from the cart then tied her to the hitching post.

"Tonight when you meet Señor Diego, at the bistro by the river, you can tell him that you are very pleased," Pedro said. He turned his cart around. "I am sure you can get her for a very good price."

As he watched Pedro ride away, he began to wonder if all of this gift giving by Diego might be drawing too much attention to the two of them. He felt somewhat uncomfortable about that.

When he turned to walk back into the house he noticed, out of the corner of his right eye, an officer on horseback three blocks away. The officer stood at the corner of St. Louis Street watching him. He wondered how long the officer had been there and if he had heard what they said. Perhaps a discussion with Diego about being a little more clandestine would be in order.

That evening at sundown Santiago saddled the horse. After he tightened the saddle, he noticed she had drunk a lot of the water. This was a good sign that she was settling in at her new home. He slowly rode on Dauphine Street and turned right onto Urseline. There he had to guide the horse over to the right side to avoid all the mud and manure in the center of the street. A gentle breeze blew most of the pungent smell away from him.

He stopped next to the fence behind Burns's house. He let himself in through the gate and tied the horse there inside the fence. He saw an older man of about sixty sitting in a rocking chair on the back porch. He walked up to him.

"I am Santiago de Barcelona, are you Señor Burns?"

"Yes I am. I thought that was your name. How did you like that horse?

"She is a very fine mount and I would like to buy her," he said.

"I am glad you like her," Burns replied.

"I will leave her here now and return in a day or two with the money."

"That will be fine," Burns replied, with a smile.

Santiago removed the saddle and blanket and placed them in the barn. He walked through the gate and waved to Burns as he turned onto the street toward Olivier's.

He could tell that the bistro was not far away, as he hear people talking and laughing. As he approached the front, there were young boys in the street singing and dancing. There were also men standing in the light of the door smoking cigars. He walked toward them.

"I am Diego Castellano at your service, my good man," a tall, somewhat rotund man said, stepping toward him.

"You are just the person I am looking for. My name is Santiago de Barcelona."

"Please won't you come in and join me?" Diego asked.

"Thank you," Santiago said.

"Roseta can we have a table in the far corner please?" Diego ordered.

"How is your mount, satisfactory I hope?" Diego asked Santiago.

"Much more than satisfactory. For a three-year-old she is very well trained," Santiago answered.

"That is very good. I am glad you are happy with her. I am sure that Don Andres Burns will be willing to sell her to you for a good price."

"If she is such a good horse, why get rid of her?" he asked.

"You see it is like this, he originally owned her, then sold her. Before the buyer could make the final payment, that man died of unexplained causes. Burns assumed ownership again."

"Poor fellow," Santiago said.

"Yes, indeed, he had many gambling debts," Diego explained.

"I left the horse at Burns's house. I will go back in one or two days with the money," Santiago stated.

"Let us have something to eat then we'll talk some business," Diego said. "The rice and beans with ham is very good here."

After they ordered their food, Diego leaned in on the table so he could talk to Santiago in a quiet voice.

"There is a matter we need to discuss up front. To make sure there is no misunderstanding between us, I will make this very plain and simple, my friend. You and I are both spies for the British Army. Our job is to document the activities of the Spanish military forces here in this city. From time to time we will deliver that information to another British contact. I am your commanding officer. As such I will give you assignments on a weekly basis. I will have final say on any questions about orders. Is that understood?" Diego asked.

"Yes, sir, absolutely," Santiago answered.

Chapter 6

As they ate, Diego consumed his food loudly and abundantly. After he finished two helpings, he ordered another glass of wine. Santiago began to think his contact was nothing more than a glutton.

"So, tell me how your passage was from Spain?" Diego asked.

"When I purchased the ticket in Cadiz, Spain, the ticket agent said it would be four weeks. When we arrived at the mouth of the river it had been six weeks and many storms," he answered.

"How much do you think Burns will want for the horse and saddle?" Santiago asked.

"I am not sure," Diego said. "But what ever it is make him a counter offer of about half that amount."

"Sounds like from what you say that he will be expecting me to come back at him with a very low bid," replied Santiago.

"The bidding should go on for a while. He lowers his price a little and you go up slightly. Continue that until you feel he may not go any lower," Diego explained.

"When we decide on a price will he want full payment then?" Santiago asked.

"He probably will, but don't worry I am authorized to advance you the full amount."

"That sounds almost too simple. How will I find you when I need that money?"

"We will meet here for supper most every night for a while. You can tell me the price on the evening of the day you make the deal. Then I will bring you that amount the next evening."

"Taking care of the horse and saddle business was easy enough," Santiago said, with a smile.

"Now, what else do you need?" Diego asked, before downing his second glass of wine.

"A gun and a knife."

"Any particular kind?"

"The knife should be about the size of the usual dirk. Something about twenty centimeters or the length from the tip of my fingers to the inside of my wrist." Santiago explained, casually in a voice that would make Diego think he knew about knives.

"I figured you for the Bowie knife type," Diego said, with a big grin.

"No not I, the Bowie is too big and hard to throw. I want something smaller; you know something with a sharp double edged blade that I can keep on my waist. The sort of thing for close in fighting," Santiago explained.

"That should be no problem, my friend."

"Now for the pistol," Santiago said. "I would like a pair of dueling pistols in the kit. Make sure it has the hammer with the ramrod. Preferably the roughed bore with the newer percussion cap that I heard of recently. And make sure it is at least a 13 mm caliber manufactured by Wogdon of London. If you cannot get that then just make it a set of the standard Spanish military flintlocks. You know, the old .72 caliber."

"My friend," Diego said smiling. "Surely you jest. Even if I could find one of those Wogdon dueling sets, the price would be prohibitive. Then there would be the rule the government here has against purchasing English made items. And, if you were caught with it, you would surely be accused of spying for the British army."

"You are right," Santiago replied. "I will be happy with the Spanish pistol. At least with it the soldiers will not accuse me spying."

"Then very good, my friend," Diego said. "Hopefully by tomorrow night you will have your horse and saddle and I will bring your gun and knife."

"I look forward to that."

"Now I must go, for you see I have another stop to make tonight. One involving a very pleasurable experience," Diego said, with a grin.

As Santiago walked back to his rent house, he thought *how nice it would be to ride a horse back to his rent house. On a horse, I could take one of the other streets that do not go through the center of town, and avoid the unpleasant smell.*

Chapter 7

Pedro said to the boy, "Now wait here by da cart. We stay on dis side of da corner til Santiago come walking by. Den you will go up to him and talk to him bout being his servant boy."

"How will I know him?" Philipe asked.

"I will point him out to you," he answered. "But, you had better not tell him dat we talked, understand?"

"Okay, I promise."

"Good, now if I can get you dis job, den you will be able to pay me back the one peso you owe me," Pedro demanded.

"Oh yeah, I almost forgot about that."

"Do not tell me dat. You are too young to be forgetful," Pedro said, squinting at him.

"Will you be here while I talk to him?"

"No, I will take the cart to run some errands for da officers," Pedro explained. "I will be in da usual place later. Come and find me den to tell me how you made out."

"I will."

"Okay, here he comes, da tall fellow with dark hair on de oter side of de street. De one wit the shiny riding boots," Pedro whispered.

"Now?" Philipe asked with a slightly trembling voice.

"Yea, go now," Pedro said, as he turned the horse and the cart around.

As Philipe walked across the street, he turned his head back to look at Pedro. He was already in the next block.

"Oh, Señor," Philipe said loudly. "I am thirteen years old and a good man servant."

"How can someone be a man servant when he is only thirteen?" Santiago asked, looking down at the boy with great curiosity.

"Even though am young, I got much experience."

"Now, I find it hard to believe that a boy your age has much experience at anything," he said, as he stopped to look down at him again.

Philipe shot back at him quickly, "I's knows how to take care of clothes and shine your boots, clean your saddle and give oats and water to your horse."

"I am on my way to see Señor Burns about a horse and do not have time for this."

"Oh, I can help you bring the horse back to your house," Philipe said, in an excited voice. "I am good stable boy!"

At this point, Santiago was continuing to walk along and Philipe was walking, almost running, to keep up with him.

"Please Señor, I work cheap and don't take up much room. I have no place to live and hardly anything to eat. I have no father and my mother died of the smallpox. See, here is my vaccination," he explained, as he rolled up his sleeve and showed him the mark.

"I have told you already, you are not big enough," Santiago said, in a frustrated tone.

"If I don't find a job I will just die in this place," Philipe said, sobbing as he sat down in the mud and manure in the middle of the street.

Santiago turned and looked back at him. He could see his long, tussled brown hair hanging over his ears and into his blue eyes. Tears were streaming down his cheeks.

Santiago stopped. For a moment he looked at him.

"Alright," he said, in a exasperated tone. "You can work for me. After all, it is a big house."

"Oh yea," Philipe yelled, as he jumped up out of the mud and muck and ran over to Santiago and threw his arms around his legs.

"Alright, alright," Santiago said, as he peeled the young lad off of him.

"Let's go now to see Señor Burns," he explained. "Your first job is going to be with the horse."

"Yes, sir," Philipe said with a smile.

Santiago paid approximately the price he wanted for the horse. It and the saddle turned out to be more than he hoped for.

"I have never seen a horse as fine as this one," exclaimed Philipe, as they both rode it back to the house.

"Do you have any of your belongings to pick up before we get to the house?" Santiago asked.

"Uh, no, sir. Everything I own is on my back," he said quietly.

"That is not a problem my man," Santiago explained, "I will send you over to Señor Caraby the tailor. I will have him fix you up with a couple of pairs of pants and shirts. If you are going to work for me you have to look like a man's man."

"Oh, I have never had a new pair of pants and shirt," Philipe said breathlessly.

As the horse slowly plodded along Philipe suddenly had a feeling of happiness and security, something he had never felt before.

"Tonight, I will meet Diego at the bistro for supper and you will find some bacon in the kitchen for yourself. Tomorrow night I will be at home so I will need to find someone to bring us in some food," Santiago explained.

They arrived at the front of the house and dismounted.

"I will take her to the back and remove the saddle," Philipe said in an excited tone.

"Whoa, slow down," Santiago interrupted. "We do not have a barn in the back. So, will be using that old carriage house there on the right."

"Okay, then that will be perfect," Philipe said.

Chapter 8

As Santiago rode up to the front of the bistro, he could see Diego's horse already at the hitching post. When he dismounted leaving his horse at the post, he glanced back over his shoulder at the Mexican saddle. The silver on the large horn made him think it may not be such a good idea to leave it out in this part of the town unattended. He thought to himself, *Next time I will bring Philipe along to watch it.*

Diego was sitting at a table all alone over in the far corner away from the door.

"Your friend is already two glasses ahead you," Roseta said with a smile.

"By now he will be ready to eat and not talk so much," Santiago suggested.

"Hello, my friend, please have a seat," Diego said.

With a smile he motioned to Roseta, "Bring, my friend, a glass of that wine and me one also."

"You sound like you are in good spirits tonight," Santiago said.

"That is true, my friend," Diego explained.

Santiago looked around the room at the customers.

"I do not see any military types in here tonight," he said.

"Nothing serious going on here," Diego laughed as he answered.

They both had the chicken with rice and beans and several glasses of wine. After they finished the meal, they moved their plates to the side and Diego gave Santiago a good Cuban cigar. As they smoked, they talked about the military units in the city.

"First there is the Louisiana Infantry Regiment commanded by Coronel Pedro Pardon. It consists of six companies of about one hundred men each. These men are primarily from Catalonia. You may know some of them," Diego began quietly. "They are the professional soldiers and primarily white."

"You are right; I got to know some of them in Barcelona during my training," Santiago explained.

"Next there are two regiments of local militia made up of libres, free men of African descent. One is the so-called Pardos or light skinned and the other is the Morenos or dark skinned," Diego said.

"I observed some of the Pardos in action when I disembarked from the ship," Santiago said.

"Chasing after cimarrones no doubt," Diego remarked quickly.

Santiago asked, "Cimarrones, what are they?"

"They are the runaway slaves," Diego explained. "Coronel Pardon's officers use those two units primarily for capturing runaway slaves."

"That kind of activity probably does not require a lot of training," Santiago stated.

"That is correct. You will not see them training in any formation very often," Diego said quietly. "Now for the Louisiana Regiment, that is a different story. This latter group will be doing some kind of training exercise almost everyday."

"Thank you for that information. I will look for the Louisiana Regiment during my observations," he whispered.

"Do you have a good location for that?" Diego asked.

"Yes, a very good one. From my second story bedroom window I can see the open area by the barracks on Toulouse Street," Santiago answered quietly.

"How about anything else there?" Diego asked.

"Oh yes, there is, as a matter of fact. It is the powder magazines across the field from those barracks," he said.

"How did you know those buildings were powder magazines?" Diego asked. "After all they look like any other building here in town. And there is no sign on them."

"Your man, Pedro, told me so on the day I arrived," Santiago said, with a proud grin.

Diego looked at him with a smile for a few seconds and then said, "Oh, so you tricked him into telling you that. I think you are very crafty, my friend. That is good."

"Thank you," Santiago said. "I think you and I should very careful about the information we share with him."

"I agree," Diego said. "During your observations be sure to make good notes, my friend."

"I will make a point of that," Santiago answered.

"Tell me how did you make out buying the horse from Burns?" Diego asked.

"Very well actually," he responded. "I got him to come down to one hundred pesos. While I was paying him, I noticed an officer sitting on Burns's porch. I am not sure what to make of that."

Santiago was interrupted by several men speaking loudly that came into the bistro.

He and Diego looked toward the loud voices. They could see the four men were in uniform, seating themselves, not far from the bar.

"Let us meet here again in two days at the same time. Then I will have some cash for you," Diego said, just above a whisper. They both slowly stood up as not to draw attention and walked toward the door.

"I am glad to hear you had a good voyage, my friend," he said loudly so the officers could hear. He patted Santiago on the back while they walked through the door.

Outside they mounted their horses and Diego waved as he slowly rode west along the river.

Chapter 9

Early the next morning Santiago awoke just before sunrise with the first crowing of the rooster. He very quietly, and without lighting a candle, put on his shirt and pants, but not his boots. Walking softly he crossed the room to the armoire and carefully removed his telescope from its hiding place. After that, he again carefully and slowly walked to the window facing the backyard and Toulouse Street by the barracks. Very slowly he moved the curtain open, slightly, in the center of the window. Yet was enough to be able to put the end of the telescope between the curtains. Gently he adjusted the focus so that the sentries came into sharp view. He watched as the ones on the outside perimeter slowly walked their assigned positions. There were four of them. More were standing at parade rest in front of the commandant's office at the far end of the block. In his small notebook, he made note of the number and location of the sentries. He included a drawing of the installation.

Now the sun was beginning to rise in the east and he thought it best to stop at this point. He returned the telescope to its original position inside the armoire along with the notebook. He had loosened one of the boards in the back enough to slip both the telescope and notebook behind it. That way if anyone opened the door they would not be able to see the hiding place. He repeated this procedure several times per day, being careful not to be discovered.

"Time to get up and feed the horse," he said to Philipe while sticking his head into the room just off from the dining area.

"Do I get my new pants and shirt today?" Philipe asked even before getting out of bed.

"Yes, of course."

"When do we go there?" Philipe inquired, while putting on his worn out shoes.

"First you have to feed the horse like I told you already, then we eat something and then we saddle the horse and ride down to the tailor shop."

"Do you think I can get some new shoes too?"

"Of course."

"Alright now I feed the horse," Philipe said as he walked out the door.

Widow Tourneur had left some flour and bacon behind from her visit. Santiago made the best of his limited cooking skills and whipped up some biscuits and bacon. They both ate well, or so he thought.

"How was breakfast?" Santiago asked, as they mounted the horse.

"It was better than starving," Philipe answered.

Santiago looked at him askance for a moment, and then they rode on.

At the tailor shop Santiago paid for the clothes in advance. He left Philipe there with instructions to bring the clothes home immediately afterwards.

After leaving the tailor shop, he rode on the River Road in the direction of the Bore plantation. He stopped just short of the Chapitoula settlement, dismounted and slowly looked at the country side. Then, he slowly returned to the city. This ride would be enough to convince anyone who was watching him of his sincerity in searching for plantation land.

For the first time in his life, Philipe was doing exactly as he was told. There was something about being given a fine gift that made him want to show respect and do the right thing.

Walking on Dumain Street was not easy for Philipe. He had to carry the package and side-step all the muck. To make it home with the package of new clothes was the only objective for him today.

When he approached Royale Street, he spotted Pedro on the other side of the intersection. Pedro saw him too. Philipe stopped by the de Lanzos' house. Pedro came toward him across the intersection.

"Hello dere, Señor Philipe," he said in a surly tone. "I see yous got de job so where dat peso?"

Philipe was two heads smaller than Pedro. He remembered from their first meeting that Pedro was a bully.

"You'll get it when I get paid!" he shot back at Pedro.

"What in dat package?" Pedro asked as he reached for it.

Philipe was just a little bit faster and pulled back away from him.

"None of your business!" He said.

Pedro lunged and Philipe hit the wall of the house. Pedro grabbed the package and tore one side open.

"Oh new clothes eh, maybe I keep some."

Philipe jumped up on Pedro's back, grabbed the package and knocked Pedro down in the process. As soon as Philipe's feet hit the ground, with package in hand, he started to run for the street.

"I get you for dis," he heard Pedro say as he came after him. As soon as Philipe turned around, he stumbled over a large pile of dried horse manure. The package hit the ground. He looked up and saw Pedro about two paces behind. Philipe grabbed the top half of the dried manure. With all his strength he threw it at Pedro. The whole smelly mass hit Pedro square in the face, knocking the surprised Pedro to the ground.

Philipe immediately picked up the package and ran across the street. In the process, he just barely missed a pair of mules pulling a wagon. On the other side, were a couple of boys. Both were clapping, yelling, and patting him on the back as he went by.

He made it to the intersection Dauphine Street, he stopped running and began a slow walk to the house. He felt safe now.

He remembered how bad the breakfast tasted. He thought *how nice it would be to have a cook for the house.* Then he thought up a plan to get one.

Chapter 10

In the afternoon Santiago made his way back to the house. That route took him along the river where there were many ships anchored. Each flew a flag from a different country. There was Spain of course, Portugal and Venezuela, to name a few. He noted all of them by entering the information in his notebook.

Now he was hungry and thinking about eating some more of the bacon from that morning. He felt satisfied knowing he had cooked for himself and had not had to hire a cook.

"Philipe, I am back," he yelled, as he entered the house.

"Oh good you are home," Philipe answered, as he came out of the dining area.

"Come, sit down at the table. Supper is almost ready," Philipe said.

"You cooked something?" Santiago asked, with great surprise. "I was not aware you could cook. This may be interesting, or maybe not."

Santiago did as he was asked to do. He went into the dining area to the table and found it was all set for one person. He pulled back the chair and seated himself with his back to the door leading out to the kitchen. A few moments passed and there was no food.

"I am ready any time you are," he called to Philipe.

There was no answer. Then, suddenly, a plate with boiled chicken, rice and beans was placed in front of him. The hand that served it looked unfamiliar and the arm was covered down to the wrist by beautiful pink material with lace around the end. He looked up quickly and jumped to his feet. In front of him was a young lady.

"Who are you and what are you doing here?" he asked in a loud voice.

"My name is Juliana, and I am your cook," she answered shyly.

Being in the business he was in, he did not like surprises, especially with strangers in his own house.

"Cook! I do not need a cook and I did not ask for one! I can cook very well by myself, thank you," Santiago retorted loudly.

She meekly bowed in front of him and said, "But, sir, I am experienced in all kinds of food: fish, beef, goat, deer, opossum, crawfish and shrimp."

"Strange that you should all of the sudden appear here on this particular day," he muttered under his breath.

"Sir," she said, "You look very hungry. Why don't you sit down and taste the chicken. I made it with several different spices and it is very tasty."

"Yes, but first I want to get to the bottom of this," he said, with a much calmer voice.

"PHILIPE get in here!" he yelled.

"Yes, master," he said, as he quickly entered the room and bowed.

Santiago looked at him with surprise at the speed at which he appeared.

"During all this time have you been hiding just outside the door to the dining room and listening to everything being said?" Santiago asked sternly.

"Yes, master," Philipe replied.

"Perhaps you can explain this situation?" Santiago asked, in a demanding tone.

Philipe stood there silent.

"Come on, tell me, what is the meaning of all this," Santiago asked, in a cross examining tone. "Who is this girl, where did she come from and why didn't you discuss this with me first?"

"Sir, this nice man, who said he was your friend, told her to work for you as a cook," Philipe answered.

"Tell me young man, does this friendly Good Samaritan have a name?"

"It was that man Diego," Philipe said loudly and quickly.

"Oh yes, of course, good ol' jolly Diego," Santiago replied.

They were all silent for a few seconds.

"Perhaps my master would like to sit at the table and eat now before the food gets cold," Juliana said.

"Yes, of course," Santiago replied calmly. He sat and ate all that was on his plate. Then, he sat quietly for a moment thinking.

"I will have to admit, all of this food was very good. You may stay on as the cook," Santiago said, calmly and politely. "Do you need a place to live?"

"Yes, and the room attached to the kitchen outside will do just fine. I have already cleaned it up," Juliana replied, with a smile.

"In that case just make yourself at home," Santiago said.

As he turned to look at them, they were both grinning from ear to ear.

"I will, thank you," Juliana responded.

"Will five pesos per month be satisfactory?" Santiago asked.

"Yes, that will be more than satisfactory," Juliana said.

Juliana and Philipe cleared the table and they all retired for the evening.

Chapter 11

Again, the next morning Santiago was awakened to the roster serenade. And again, he went through the same routine with his telescope and notebook.

However, what he saw this morning was different and unexpected. A company of the Louisiana Infantry Regiment had formed up near the south end of the barracks and was marching in full dress uniform. They were heading toward the Plaza de Armas three blocks away. He wrote this in his notebook with the added notation, "Appeared to be practicing parade drill."

At the other end of the barracks a company of the Pardo militia had divided up into two's and were armed with muskets. They were being sent out by the lieutenant. This he noted as '30 goats x 2 led out of the corral for morning pasture'.

Suddenly Santiago could hear someone coming up the stairs. Quickly he placed everything into its hiding place. The foot steps stopped and there was a knock on the door.

"Señor Santiago, are you up yet?" the woman's voice asked.

He recognized Juliana's voice.

"Yes," he answered through the door while quickly pulling on his pants.

"I need to go to the Mercado and buy some eggs, flour and bacon," she said.

"That is quite alright. Do you want Philipe to go with you?" he asked, as he opened the door.

She was standing there about two feet away wearing a light blue full length dress with a hoop skirt. It was buttoned up to the neck with a white collar and long sleeves reaching to her wrist. He immediately noticed that she was bare foot.

"No, it is proper for the women of the house to go there to buy these things," Juliana answered.

"You will need some money," Santiago said, as he pulled a pouch from his waist pocket.

"Here take this," he said, handing her some coins.

"But, sir, this is very much more than I need. You have given me three pesos and six reales. The food will cost less than a peso," Juliana said, somewhat bewildered.

"Yes, I know, buy yourself some shoes while you are there," Santiago said.

"Oh, thank you very much, sir. You are very generous," she said, with much blushing.

She turned and ran down the stairs. Then stopped at the front door and looked back at him.

"I almost forgot, please tell Philipe to get me a bucket of fresh, clean water while I am gone," Juliana yelled.

Quickly, she disappeared out the door and down the street.

In the afternoon Santiago rode his horse slowly along the edge of the river. He was not far from the Plaza de Armas. There he noticed several ships at anchor with their gang planks down leading to the shore line. The area there was quite muddy so the crew of each ship had laid extra planks leading over the mud leading up onto the grassy area.

Several carts and wagons were parked there. He noticed that on the shore in front of the ship with the Spanish flag were several dark skinned men in uniform unloading barrels from the ship. They were placing them into a wagon up on the grassy area. As he drew nearer, he could see another wagon filled with barrels that had pulled away and was going up Toulouse Street toward the barracks.

Further up on the grassy area was an officer on horseback who appeared to be watching the men. He did not recognize that officer. Santiago was curious about the barrels so he began to ride closer.

"Hey, Señor," said the officer who began to yell at Santiago.

"You there on that horse, move away from those men and that ship," the officer yelled, while pointing his quirt at Santiago.

"Yes, sir," Santiago answered as he turned his horse toward the officer. "I was looking for a place to ride this afternoon, the weather is so nice."

"You cannot ride here, Señor. This area is off limits to everyone today," the officer explained.

Santiago noticed that some of the soldiers were taking a break and sitting in a grassy area not far from the gang-plank. One of them had lit a cigar and was puffing on it.

"Hey, you down there, put out that cigar! You want to blow up this whole place?!" the officer yelled very loudly.

Santiago took that as a hint to move along quickly. The officer's actions made him think that the material in the barrels was probably gun powder. After he had ridden out of sight he stopped and very quickly made note of all this in his notebook.

Santiago quickly rode back to the house. He entered it while leaving the horse outside. On the way up the stairs, he saw Philipe.

"My horse is out front, take her to the barn and take off the saddle, feed her some oats and water then curry her," he said, in a hurry.

"Oh by the way, where is Juliana?" he asked.

"She has gone back to the Mercado and will not be back until almost supper," he answered.

Philipe will take at least an hour to complete that chore. Juliana will be gone for a couple of hours. He will have time to make notes in his notebook. After he entered his room, he quickly looked out the window. Sure enough, Philipe was leading the horse to the barn. He knew the house was clear and he could get down to the real business at hand.

After finishing his notes, he reached his hand around the back of the armoire in order to pull it away from the wall slightly. As he gripped the lower part in the back, he felt something unusual on the wood. It felt as though someone had scratched something there. He pulled it out further and he could see that there on the wood was scratched a person's name.

The light there in the corner was dim and he could barely make out the spelling. Santiago held a lantern close. It was the name Celestin Glapion. He wondered who could this possibly be and why would they put their name on it? Was it a previous owner or maybe the man who built it? That answer will have to wait until a later time. Now he must get the report ready for Diego.

Later as Santiago walked down the stairs to the dining area, he spotted Philipe leaning against the door frame staring out towards the river. He walked over to him.

"Tonight, after I leave, you and Juliana stay here at the house and keep the door locked," Santiago said.

"Are you going to Olivier's again tonight?" Philipe asked, with a grin on his face.

"Yes," Santiago said, as he looked at Philipe. "Is that some how funny?"

"Oh no, Señor, but it is just that I have heard on the streets Roseta has her eye on you."

At that point, Santiago looked towards Juliana who was setting the table.

"Don't look at me," she said with a denying sound to her voice. "I didn't have anything to do with this!"

"Now let me set things straight," Santiago said, in a stern voice. "I came here to buy a plantation not to find a wife! Now let's sit down to this stew."

Chapter 12

Santiago arrived at Olivier's at the same time as Diego. He noticed that Diego's horse looked like an old worn out nag. This made him feel good about his own fine looking horse. The sight also made him wonder why Diego did not also have a good horse. Maybe he can tell me tonight.

As they entered the bistro, it had the usual appearance. Of the many tables, only about half were taken. These were mostly the ones in the dimly lit corners. They found one across the room from the door in a corner. Roseta quickly appeared at their table to take the order.

"My friends, what will you have tonight?"

Before Santiago could speak, Diego quickly spoke up in a loud voice.

"We shall just have wine and cigars tonight. Santiago and I will be talking about some plantations."

She answered with a smile, "Very good then," and turned and walked back to the bar.

After they lit their cigars with the table candle, Diego asked him about his activities over the last few days. Santiago told him about the men and their units at the barracks. Then he talked about the ship unloading the powder at the river.

"This is surprising. They received an identical shipment three weeks ago," Diego stated in a hushed voice. "Continue on."

"I was chased away by a teniente on horseback. There was no name on the ship and it was flying the Spanish colors."

"It could have come from either Veracruz or Havana," Diego interjected.

"Do you think that the Admiralty in London would want to know about the fact that the Spanish are laying in military supplies in New Orleans in order to launch an invasion on them in Florida?"

Diego quietly sat back in his chair looking at him and not speaking for a moment.

"So, you think that the reason you are here doing this job is because the British want to know when and where the Spanish are going to attack them!" he said in a whisper and very big eyes.

Santiago sat silent in somewhat amazement.

"I can see that before you sailed to here your education is, how I should say it, some what incomplete," Diego said quietly while leaning forward on the table. "So, now I find it necessary to bring you up to speed on the correct definition of your assignment."

"By all means please do!" Santiago exclaimed somewhat humiliated.

"First of all let me say that I am not surprised at your lack of background preparation by the Admiralty. I have seen it before.

"Secondly, yes, you were sent here to gather information about military activities and you have been doing a good job of that. It is not the Spanish that are going to attack the British in Florida. Quite the opposite. It is the British that want to attack the Spanish here in the Florida West Parishes. It is the job of you and I to gather information about strengths and weaknesses in the Spanish position so that the Admiralty can formulate a plan for that invasion."

"But, I thought that there was a peace between these two countries and that the War declared by Spain on England in 1779 was over?" Santiago asked.

"Some think that is true, but others, like myself, know better," Diego said. "Just a couple of years ago, in 1786, the British attempted to make some forays into this area. They stopped when they realized there was a massive smallpox epidemic going on here. The same pox that killed your boy Philipe's mother. And that was also the reason, I'm sure, that you were vaccinated back there before you departed."

"Do you have any idea when they will make their move?" Santiago asked, with a tone of anger and betrayal.

"My experience has been that the Admiralty is very tight lipped about such things," Diego answered. "Try not to feel so bad, my friend. It is possible that back there, before you departed, they set you up and purposefully misled you. They did something very similar to me."

"I still find this hard to believe," he replied. "Is it not true that other countries have had their eyes set on New Orleans and the Mississippi?" Santiago queried.

"Oh yes, many," Diego began. "Let me see now there are, not only the British, but possibly the French. Many Frenchmen here, and in Paris, would like to have this place back. Then there is the British East Indies Company, which is so large and in many parts of the world, that they have a military force of their own, both soldiers and navy. You might say they are equivalent to the Mother country. They would love to have this place. Last, but not least are the rebellious slaves, here in Chapitoula and not far away in Santo Domingo, who cannot be counted out."

"Sounds like the whole world is against them," Santiago stated.

"Almost."

"Now after hearing all of that, I feel like a very small pawn on a giant chess board," Santiago said dejectedly.

"Tell Roseta to bring me another glass of wine," Santiago said, in an angry tone.

"My friend it has been a difficult evening for you. Why don't we call it a night and that will give you a chance to digest all this information along with your supper. Tomorrow in the afternoon let us meet on the north side of the town and ride our horses up the river road as though we are going to look for a plantation?"

"I could not agree more," he said as they got up and left the bistro.

Chapter 13

The next afternoon Santiago had Philipe saddle his horse. His saddle had been cleaned and the horse curried. He felt very proud of the way he and the horse looked.

It was however, very little consolation to the way he felt after his discussion with Diego the night before. Since their talk had ended, many questions concerning the motives of the British had come to his mind. Santiago felt he must bring these up to Diego today.

After mounting up, Santiago started around the house toward the street.

"I do not know when I will be back, but you and Juliana stay here at the house until then," he said to Philipe, after he went through the gate.

"Ah, there you are my good man," Diego said.

"Oh, hello, I'm glad to see you are now riding a much better horse than last evening," Santiago replied, surprised to see Diego there.

"I had to have this gal shoed yesterday and the blacksmith at the stable loaned me that other one last night. I could not pick up this one until this morning. Something about the hoofs having to be trimmed first," Diego explained.

"When I saw you on that nag last night, it gave me the idea that you might be going broke," Santiago said laughingly.

"No, no, quite the opposite. Our employer has been very generous, and I have your share. I will give it to you after we get further down the road and out of site of the town," Diego said with a smile.

They passed the wooded area where the slaves sometimes met on their days off. Santiago heard some people talking behind them. He turned to see who it was, but turned back very quickly.

Santiago said quietly under his breath, "You know I think we are being followed. I just saw two soldiers in uniform riding toward us about two blocks away."

"Maybe they are or maybe they are not," Diego answered quickly. "Let us ride along at this same pace for a while then observe them again."

"Good plan," Santiago replied.

After they rounded the big curve in the road, they were along the side of the Bore plantation. They stopped and dismounted. As they were standing in front of their horses, Diego looked around up and down the road. He saw no one coming.

"Here is your money, it is a salary for two months, more or less," Diego said to Santiago as he handed him a leather pouch.

After Santiago took it in his hand, he realized how heavy it was.

"There must be more than one hundred silver pesos in this bag," Santiago said.

After looking inside he placed it in his waist pocket.

"It is precisely four hundred plata pesos fuerte (*strong silver pesos*)," explained Diego.

Just then both of the horses whinnied and snorted, shaking their heads. The men stopped talking and looked around. They saw nothing.

Diego said quietly, "That could have been just a raccoon, but it also could have been someone checking up on us from those bushes. I am going to get my pistol out of my saddle bag. I suggest you do likewise."

Santiago was already one thought ahead of him. At that moment, he had his hand inside his own saddle bag getting out his pistol. They slipped their guns into their waist bands and slowly mounted the horses, the whole time keeping their eyes on the trees. They continued on the road talking quietly as they went.

"So, tell me, what is the reason for the great generosity of our employer?" Santiago asked.

Diego explained, "I do not know for sure, but there could be many reasons. However, in your case this is the first pay since you filed a report. Evidently they liked that report, this is their way of showing you that."

"It is nice to know I am appreciated," Santiago answered.

"But, also it is good not to look a gift horse in the mouth," Diego said.

"I hear what you say and I will keep it in mind," Santiago responded.

"This week is one of celebration," Diego began. "Monday, the seventeenth, was St. Patrick's Day. This coming Friday, the twenty-first, is Good Friday, a very religious holiday here."

"I remember, we had that religious holiday in Barcelona back home," Santiago replied.

"On Thursday night, several of, my friends and I will be having a soiree, at Olivier's. Please come and join us. There will be much food, drink and many women," Diego said with a smile.

"That sounds like great fun. I have not been to a serious party in a very long time. You can count me in," Santiago replied.

"Oh, by the way, I almost forgot," Diego said. "Remember that question you asked me about the ship full of slaves you saw on the river bank when you landed?"

"Yes, I do," Santiago answered.

"I found out more about that situation. That ship, the *Governor Miro*, had delivered one hundred and twenty-nine slaves to New Orleans from Dominica. It just so happens that they stopped over in Port Royal, about four weeks ago for provisions and for the better security that port offered. Seems the slaves were very unruly. Unfortunately, I cannot tell you who the slaves were consigned to, probably someone in Chapitoula, just up the river," Diego explained.

"Very interesting," Santiago replied. "I have not heard of any large slave sales."

"Neither have I. And I will find out more about that sooner or later," Diego said with a grin.

"It is getting late in the afternoon and we should turn back," Diego said.

"Yes, I agree," Santiago said.

After Santiago arrived at the house, he very quietly made his way upstairs to his room. He was sure that Philipe and Juliana were in the house or out in the kitchen. It was most important that they do not see him with the bag of pesos. He was sure that if they saw him, and the bag, they would ask questions.

He took the pouch containing the pesos out of his waist band and very carefully counted them. Diego was right, there were four hundred pesos in the pouch. He transferred all of them to his new pouch. It was a very nice one that he purchased from a leather shop in Cadiz, Spain, before he boarded the ship. He liked it so much that he had the shop owner sew his initials, S B, into the side of the bag. Before he put it away, he took out twenty-five pesos for spending money to carry with him every day.

Santiago stood up on the chair beside the armoire and placed the bag on top behind some books. Knowing that it was out of sight gave him a sense of security. After hiding the pouch he quietly looked out the door up and down the hall way. He went downstairs, and found no one.

He wanted to give the appearance of not having arrived yet. To accomplish this, he very quietly went out the back door and came in again through the front door.

Chapter 14

Upon entering the house that second time, he was met at the door by Philipe.

"Hello, Philipe. Did you know this is a week for celebration?" Santiago asked, as he brought in his saddlebags.

"In two days it will be Good Friday. A day off for everyone including the church," Santiago added.

"Yes, and did you know that today is the Spring Equinox?" Philipe asked.

"No, I was not aware of that, how did you know that?" Santiago asked

"There are many superstitious people in this town. Some of them are planning a meeting of sorts tonight," Philipe explained.

"Did the Urseline nuns teach you that?" Santiago asked.

"No, I heard it on the streets," Philipe answered. "They also said that Friday night we will have a full moon."

"You are a pretty smart fellow," Santiago said as a compliment.

"The nuns also taught me how to read the calendar and figure the days. This is a leap year and last month had twenty-nine days instead of the usual twenty-eight," Philipe said.

"Sounds like a lot of things for these superstitious people to get excited about," Santiago said.

"I will put the horse in the barn and then the supper should be ready," Philipe said.

As Santiago climbed the stairs, he began to think about those superstitious people that Philipe had mentioned. They worried him and at the same time reminded him of a similar group of people back home in Spain. They too did strange things during the full moon and the equinox.

Also troubling him were the two soldiers that appeared to be following them that day. He could not put his finger on it, but something about that situation seemed out of place.

At the party on the night before Good Friday, Santiago was late and when he got there, he found that the drinking had already begun. Santiago found Diego at a table in the back of the room, with Roseta. Diego was already three sheets to the wind.

"Oh look who finally made it," Diego exclaimed. "We were not sure you were coming so we started without you. We felt you would not mind."

"I can always catch up to you if I wanted to," Santiago answered.

"That is the spirit," Diego yelled, with a slurred voice and then laughed.

The whole place was full to capacity with every table taken and people standing along the wall and at the bar.

Just then, two waitresses came out of the kitchen with trays of boiled shrimp, rice and crawfish. They set them on the bar and everyone began to gather around. By the time he and Diego stood up, there were so many people around the trays that they could not see them.

"We had better get over there and get our share or we may go hungry," Diego said laughingly.

The evening was a complete success. Many friendly strangers were there and all had a good time.

Santiago did not drink very much and with good reason. Diego, it was obvious, had already taken in way too much. Santiago was prepared to take him outside if he started to talk about sensitive information.

Santiago did not let Diego get out of earshot all evening. Roseta kept looking at Santiago during that time. She had an angry look on her face.

Several hours later, Santiago helped Diego to his horse, making sure he rode away from the bistro. Santiago went back inside, bought a bottle of wine and found Roseta. The bistro was almost empty and they were together. Now she had a smile on her face.

They found a little table outside in the moonlight. Both drank the wine and talked until closing. Santiago wanted to stay with her, but he was very tired and wanted to sleep. He kissed her goodnight and promised to see her the next day. Very slowly, the horse found its way back to the house, with Santiago asleep in the saddle.

Chapter 15

As Santiago slept, he dreamed of the time when he was younger. In this dream he walked among the sunny vineyards his family worked just south of Barcelona. Most of all, he remembered the smell and the feel of the soft Mediterranean breezes and the sense of well-being it gave him. In this dream, he longed for those days when his life was simpler and not so complicated.

He also dreamed of the party the night before. It was such a wonderful time, he felt as though he was still at the party. There was so much good food and drink, not to mention all the pretty women. Roseta looked lovely and it was so nice to be able to spend time with her. He wished he could have stayed longer. Maybe he would get another chance to see her alone.

Suddenly, in the distance, he heard a loud noise like a cannon firing. Slowly waking up, he thought, *What a headache, I must still be drunk. It is only the army practicing.*

He rolled over and went back to his dream of Roseta's pretty face. Soon he began to hear someone off in the distance calling his name. He thought *My mother must be calling me for supper.*

The calling became louder and suddenly Philipe came bursting in through the bedroom door.

"SEÑOR SANTIAGO, SEÑOR SANTIAGO!" Philipe yelled, breathlessly at the top of his voice,

"There is a battle going on outside."

Santiago sat up on the side of his bed and put his hands on Philipe's small shoulders.

"Relax, my young friend, it is only the army having artillery practice," he said, with a slurred voice.

Just at that moment, there were two more loud explosions, in rapid succession. The floor in the bedroom shook violently. Both he and Philipe fell off the bed and onto the floor. The two looked at each other then quickly jumped to their feet.

"Look out the window and you will see what I mean," Philipe said, voice trembling.

Santiago, also shaking, pulled back the curtain and looked out the window.

"The whole city is on fire! There is so much smoke that I cannot see the barracks on Royale Street," Santiago said.

Santiago looked out the window into the neighbor's yard and saw the sun dial.

"It is almost two in the afternoon. Hand me my boots while I put on my pants," Santiago said to Philipe.

After he dressed they both ran down the stairs. When they reached the bottom step Santiago tripped, but was able to break his fall with his hands. Looking down at his feet, he realized he had his boots on the wrong feet. Quickly he changed them and out the front door onto Dauphine Street they went.

"We must find widow Tourneur. Philipe, do you know where she is?" Santiago asked.

"This morning, she said she was going to spend this Good Friday holiday with her friend. But, I do not know where her friend lives," Philipe answered.

"We will not be able to find her if we do not know which house she is in. She may already be dead. Let us go around the corner to our right and look down Saint Peter Street," Santiago said.

When Santiago turned the corner, he immediately stopped.

"I cannot believe what I am seeing. Look, two blocks away, the fire is already across Royale Street and headed this way," Santiago said.

"The church and the prison are completely on fire," Philipe said.

"Yes, and over to the right, on the corner of Royal and Toulouse, some of the army barracks are on fire. Hell is coming to take us. I can feel the heat. We have got to get out of here and fast. Quick, help me get my horse from the stable," Santiago ordered Philipe.

As they ran to the stable, they heard the loud roaring noise made by the flames.

"I can hear a lot of people screaming and calling for help. Maybe we should stay and help them," Philipe said.

"Philipe, my hands are shaking so much I cannot get the saddle tightened. Come here and help me," Santiago ordered, in a shaky voice.

"Let me help you with that strap. Where will you go?" Philipe asked.

"We will go out the St. Jean Gate, two blocks to the right, then turn to the left to the River Road, then as far as possible," Santiago yelled.

"Señor your face is very pale and your eyes are wide. You do not seem like yourself. We should stay and help those people who have been hurt," Philipe yelled, staring at Santiago in disbelief.

Wind began to blow much harder and the roaring sound of the flames much louder.

"If we stay here we will die like all those other people," Santiago yelled, mounting up on his saddle.

"Come on get up here behind me and let's go," Santiago said, reaching down and taking Philipe by his left arm.

"No! I don't want to go. I want to stay here with my people. I want to go and help them," Philipe said, pulling back from Santiago.

"If you do not come with me you will surely die like all the rest of them. The fire is too big. It is every man for himself. Now, get on and let's go before this horse throws me," Santiago yelled hysterically.

"I thought you were a strong person, but now I think you are a coward. You are running away at the first sign of trouble," Philipe said, as the horse jumped back and he pulled away from Philipe and ran out the barn door with Santiago on her back.

Santiago watched as Philipe turned right and ran on St. Peter Street. Santiago followed him on horseback until Philipe disappeared onto Bourbon Street a block away.

He turned his horse and rode through the St. Jean Gate.

The horse run at a full gallop for about ten minutes. Then he slowed his her to a walk.

As the horse walked for a while, he began to relax. From behind, he could hear the roaring noise of the fire and occasional screams of the people. He stopped his horse and turned in his saddle to look back at the city. He thought to himself, *I have not lived here very long and these are not my people. Why should I risk my neck for them?*

He stared at the inferno, with its smoke billowing in a dark brown color and occasional burst of orange red flames. He turned back around in the saddle and continued riding his horse at a walk.

Five minutes later, he stopped again. And again Santiago turned and looked at the fire. Then he looked at the ground and when he did, a powerful feeling came over him. A feeling he had not felt since he was a boy in Barcelona. It was when he was caught stealing apples from a street vendor's cart. The feeling was shame and guilt.

Suddenly he remembered something his cousin Tomas, the priest, told him when he was a teenager: *Love thy neighbor as thyself.*

He thought to himself, *If I go back there I can help some of those people. It is not right for me to run away and think only of myself. Their lives are just as important as mine, maybe even more so.*

Without thinking about it, he turned his horse back toward the town. He hit his horse with his quirt repeatedly and it responded by jumping up and taking off at a full gallop.

The city with its fire and smoke came into complete view as he turned by the northwest corner of the city. On to Bienville Street and then to the river. He rode quickly along the shore line passed several soldiers guarding boxes of supplies.

The next site he encountered took his breath away.

Chapter 16

There appeared to Santiago to be more than a thousand people gathered by the river. Some standing and staring in disbelief. Others crying with tears streaming down their cheeks. There were the mothers holding their children to their side as they all cried together. They all had come to this point by the river to seek relief from the heat of the fire.

He turned the corner to go north on St. Philippe Street and he could see the fire out of the corner of his left eye. He felt the heat on the left side of his body and face. There were people moving toward him, some walking others running. He was going against the flow, a mass of humanity headed for the river.

He yelled out to some as they walked by, "Has anyone seen widow Tourneur?"

No one answered. He called out again, "Widow Tourneur, has anyone seen her?"

Still no answer. He stood up off his saddle pushing himself up with his feet in the stirrups looking out over the people as they made their way towards him. His horse, which had been unbelievably still during this time, made a sharp turn to the right almost throwing him out of the saddle.

"Señor Santiago, Señor Santiago," a voice said.

Santiago looked down in amazement. It was Philipe, holding one of the reins.

Philipe said, "Yes, it is me, master."

"I am so glad to see you are alive, "Santiago replied, as he dismounted.

"Have you seen the widow Tourneur?" Santiago asked.

"No," Philipe replied in a harsh voice.

"What happened to your voice?" Santiago asked.

"I breathed in some smoke awhile ago," Philipe explained.

"Come get on behind me and we will ride to the end of the street beyond the fire," Santiago said, "This wind out of the south is beginning to blow harder. It will push the fire very fast and we must go now to get ahead of it."

After Santiago mounted his horse, he pulled Philipe up behind him on the saddle. He wrapped his arms around Santiago very tightly.

Santiago said, "Don't worry, I won't let you fall off."

"It is not the falling off that scares me," he said. "The fire, it is so hot and moving so fast, that is what scares me. And, I have no family, no mother, father, no brother or sister. I am all alone except for you. When you rode out of town on your horse, I got so scared, and thought I would never see you again. You are all the family I have."

At that point, Santiago was silent for a few moments as they slowly walked the horse toward the end of the street. He thought to himself, how guilty and ashamed he was for his actions. Now, he must do the right thing.

"How foolish it was of me to lose my head and let the fear take a hold of my mind," he told Philipe.

He turned around in the saddle and put his arm around Philipe and while looking him in the eye said, "From now on I will be your father."

They looked at each other, and smiled.

"It is very close to us now and going faster than I expected. The wind is blowing the flames and embers over onto their next door neighbors' houses," Santiago said, in a hurried voice.

"What should we do now?" Philipe asked.

"We need to find widow Tourneur. It looks like the fire is moving in that direction. Maybe we can save some of her effects from the house. Get up on the horse with me, so we can ride to her house."

Philipe held on tightly as Santiago made the horse go as fast as possible.

"Look, there she is at the house," Philipe said, as they got closer.

Santiago stopped the horse quickly and they jumped off.

"We will help you move out some of the furniture," Santiago said, hurriedly.

The widow was standing in the yard of the house next door with a very frightened look on her face.

"Santiago, I am so glad you are here," she said.

"We must move quickly if we are going to save any of your furniture," he said.

"It is too late for that," she replied. "The fire is now coming across Bourbon Street, and it is about to get Jacques Martine's house. It is the one just behind us."

"He has the young wife and sons, does he not?" Santiago asked.

"Yes," widow Tourneur answered. "And I have not seen them today."

They walked around the side of her house. What they saw confirmed their worst fears. The roof of the Martine's house was already on fire.

"I hear someone yelling," Philipe said.

"So, do I, and it sounds like it is coming from inside their house," widow Tourneur said. "We had better get there fast."

"Look the fire is on the entire roof," Philipe said, as they ran across the lot towards the Martine's house.

As they approached the back of the house a boy of about ten years came out.

"Come help me quick my mother has fallen and I can't get her up," he yelled.

"Show us where she is, so we can to get her out quickly," Santiago said.

"She is by the window at the end of the stairs. You hold the door open, and I will pick her up and carry her out," Santiago said.

"This smoke is starting to burn my eyes and my throat," Santiago said, as he carried her out into the backyard.

"Santiago move Mrs. Martine to the yard beside my house. This wind is blowing much harder now and it will not long before those burning pieces of the shingles land on my house," The widow Tourneur said.

Philipe asked the boy, "What is your name?"

"Jon," he said.

"Jon, did your father go to his bakery today?" Widow Tourneur asked Jon.

"No, today is a holiday so he stayed home," Jon said. "A little while ago, after the fire started, he left to go get someone to help us with the furniture. He has not come back. My mother was very worried and she cried when he did not return right away."

"She is still breathing," Santiago said, as he carried her quickly across the lot. "Somebody get some water to put on her face."

They reached the back of widow Tourneur's house and Santiago laid Mrs. Martine down on the green grass by the back door.

Santiago said quietly to widow Tourneur, "As I laid her down my hand rubbed against the back of her head. I felt a lump about the size of a walnut."

"That must have happened when she fell down the stairs," she suggested.

"She is still unconscious," Santiago said, in a concerned tone.

Just then, as Jon turned around and looked at his house, he screamed, "OH NO!"

"What is it?" Santiago asked.

They all looked back, "Mother of God," the widow said. "All the houses on Bourbon Street are on fire now," then she crossed herself.

Santiago said, "I must go inside and quickly get some of my effects. Then we must leave this place."

He ran into the widow Tourneur's house, up the stairs to his bedroom, and retrieved the monocular looking glass he had won from Angus, and the small notebook. Running down the stairs, he realized that he had forgotten the money pouch. Quickly he returned to the room and grabbed the pouch, dropping two coins on the floor in the process. He did not take time to pick them up, but continued out the front door almost as fast as he went in.

"Hook up the horse to that cart and we will take Mrs. Martine with us," Santiago said to Philipe, while pointing to the small two wheel cart

"Let's go now, this wind is very strong and the embers from the Martine's house are starting to fall onto our roof," he said, shouting loudly over the noise.

The roaring sounds of the fire and the gale force wind made normal conversation impossible.

"I must save some of my nice furniture," the widow screamed in a hysterical voice.

"Are you crazy? Don't go in there," Santiago yelled.

She did not hear him and started making her way to the door. Just as she was about to step up the small stairs he grabbed her around the waist and started carrying her toward the cart.

"Philipe, get the horse and cart out into the road," Santiago yelled.

"The roof is now on fire," Philipe yelled.

"I see it. Keep moving," Santiago yelled. "Those embers are starting to fall on us so don't stop for anything."

Jon Martine and his mother were in the back of the cart as Santiago approached with the widow. He put her on the cart next to the boy. Tears were streaming down her face as she stared back at the house.

The flames were now coming out of the second story windows. In just a matter of moments, the house was consumed by the orange red monster. She could look no longer and buried her face into her hands.

The horse began to stop and rear up and almost tipped the wagon over backwards.

"Hold the horse tight while I take off my shirt. I will wrap it around the horse's face to cover the eyes," Santiago commanded.

Santiago looked up into the sky. There between the billows of smoke, he could see dark storm clouds beginning to form.

Chapter 17

Santiago said, "There is the lot. It already has some other horses and cows."

"Is this the one that Señor Andres Burns bought?" Philipe asked.

"Yes, that is it exactly," Santiago answered.

As they drew closer to the lot the roaring sound and the smell of the smoke from the burning cypress lumber lessened. However, the strong wind continued to blow embers over their heads. The embers landed in the empty fields across Dauphine Street igniting grass fires.

Finally, the cart stopped. Santiago removed the blindfold from the horse's eyes. After he did that, she drew closer to the others. Mrs. Martine began to move around.

"What am I doing here?" she asked in a panic.

"Oh Mom," Jon yelled.

Suddenly she rose up and seeing where she was, became confused. She leapt down from the cart as though she was going to run.

"Augh," she yelled, and fell face first onto the street that was ankle deep in very wet mud and manure. They rushed over and picked her up and put her back on the cart.

"Oh Mom," Jon said. "You have all that smelly stuff all over you."

"Here, I will take off my shirt and dip it in the watering trough and help you get clean," Jon said.

"I was so dizzy, everything is spinning around," Mrs. Martine said. "What has happened?"

"We got you out of the house and Señor Santiago carried you to widow Tourneur's," Philipe said hurriedly.

"Do you remember falling down the stairs and hitting your head as we were about to leave the house?" Jon asked.

"I have this awful pain in the back of my head," Mrs. Martine answered.

"You have a pretty good bump back there and you were out for a while. What happened to the other people in your house?" Santiago asked

She looked at him with a slightly confused look.

Then she answered, "I think my husband and younger son left the house before lunch."

"That is correct, Mom," Jon answered.

"What about the five slaves?" Santiago asked.

For a moment, she was quiet. Then she said, "Oh, now I remember, today is a holiday so all of them had the day off. On those days they will go to that area just outside the city they call 'Congo'."

"I'm sure they all got away from the fire and are okay," Santiago said.

The widow Tourneur stepped out of the cart stood up on the ground, and looked in the direction of the center of town.

"Look the wind is still blowing hard, but the fire is out now on the east side of the city," she said.

They all looked in that direction. The area which used to be large houses was now just smoldering ashes.

"Now the fire is raging on the north end of town and also over in the west side between Dauphine and Bourbon Streets," Santiago added.

They all began to relax a little and were relieved to know they had just out run the fire and were still alive.

Each got some water to drink out of the horse trough. All the animals inside the fence had gathered in a tightly packed group along the fence on the east side, farthest away from the flames. The horses watched closely making sure that there would be some water left for them.

As the wind continued to whip the smoke around a few towns' people began to gather at the horse lot. They were in small groups of three, four. Some could be heard softly speaking in French, others in Spanish.

Then one man leaning on the fence around the corner next to the road asked in a loud voice, "Savez-vous si quelqu'un est mort dans cet incendie?" (*Do you know if anyone died in this fire?*). They all stood there silently shaking their heads.

The events of this day had transpired at a very rapid pace. So fast that most had lost track of the time.

Santiago looked upward and shading the bright sun from his eyes exclaimed, "It looks like we have about one hour of sunlight left before it gets dark."

The widow Tourneur put her hands on both sides of her face and said, "Oh my God what will we do tonight?"

Turning to the others of her little group and with eyes wide open in fright said, "We have no home; no place to sleep, no food to eat, no clothes to wear."

Santiago said, "We should go back to your house now and see what remains.

Chapter 18

They watered the horse, turned the cart around and headed back on Dauphine Street from which they came. They slowed as they entered the area where the fire had been.

"Philipe walk the horse and the cart far over to the right side of the road," Santiago said.

"Look at all the people behind us," Philipe stated after looking back. "There is no one in front of us so we must be the leader."

"Yes, my friend, someone must lead and someone must follow," Santiago said.

"These houses burned so fast. From the looks of these houses, the people will not be able to save any of their effects," widow Tourneur said.

As they approached the place where the Tourneur's house once stood, they slowly came to a stop. After a few moments they led the horse and cart on to the lot next to where the house had been. It was an area of very little grass, and away from the smoldering and timbers.

The widow stood by the cart looking at what was left of her house while fighting back the tears.

She said, "This house was everything to me. It was my place to live, a place for my children and it also provided me with an income. Now it is all gone."

She stood there with one hand on her hip and the other covering her eyes and her head bowed.

"You are a strong woman Mrs. Tourneur," Santiago said, as he put his hand on her shoulder. "I know you will be able to start over."

"Start over! I am old, I have seen sixty-one years. It took my husband and me years to make this place our home. He is dead and gone, the children are grown and moved away and now the house is gone.

"And here I am all alone with no house, no money, no food and no place to sleep," she lamented. She took a few steps and sat on a tree stump in the grass.

"Santiago," she asked, with her face still in her hands. "What are we going to do now?"

"Good evening," a deep voice from behind them said. "My name is Teniente Pedro Verde of the Louisiana Infantry Regiment, under the command of Coronel Don Pedro Pardon, and we have been ordered to distribute these military tents to those whose homes have burned. If you will please be so kind as to show my men where to place it."

"Please put it over here," the widow Tourneur said, pointing to an area about ten feet from the burned house.

"This is such a wonderful thing you have done for us, you are a God send," she stated, gladly.

Suddenly, she was more like her old self again.

Santiago hurriedly called to Philipe, "Come help me to put up this tent.

Where can we get some food?" Santiago asked Verde.

Verde looked at him quietly for a moment.

"There may be some rice, flour and beans issued possibly tonight. However, it will probably be tomorrow. You see most of the food that was in the warehouses was destroyed in the fire," Verde explained.

The slaves and the soldiers pulled down a large military tent folded up and tied with rope. It took about twenty minutes to completely set it up and drive in the stakes. To the five of them it was like a castle.

"Thank you, sir," Santiago said.

"You are quite welcome," Verde said.

Verde and his men continued with the wagon on to the next house.

Jon Martine said, "My mom keeps falling asleep, and then after a little while she wakes up."

"Now that we have the tent raised, we will put her in with us for the night," widow Tourneur said. "Maybe tomorrow, if she is not better, we will look for the doctor named Derom."

Santiago stood by the road for a moment watching the soldiers and the wagon go down the street.

Philipe walked over from the tent, stood by him, and said, "What is it that you are looking at, Señor?"

"That officer looked very familiar. Do you know him?" Santiago asked.

"Oh, Don Pedro Verde. Yes, he is a good man," Philipe said. "I know that he is from Catalonia."

Then Santiago remembered the time just after he had joined the army in Barcelona. One of the tenientes in his regiment during his early training was Verde. He did not say this to Philipe or the others, but kept it to himself.

Santiago, Philipe and Jon Martine all helped widow Tourneur finish moving the small amount of personal effects she had left into the tent.

The person delivering the food did not show up that night. They all were exhausted and went to sleep in the tent soon after sun down.

Santiago did not sleep in the tent. Instead stayed out side near the cart. He lay on his saddle blanket with his head on his saddle and looked up to the stars. His fatigue slowly melted into sleep.

Chapter 19

The next morning the sun began to show itself over the tree tops. The warm rays fell on many people slowly looking through the piles of ashes and charred wood. The previous morning these had been their homes.

They talked among themselves in low voices. From time to time the sound of someone crying.

As he stood up from his saddle blanket Santiago felt the pain in his lower back from sleeping on the ground. He took a deep breath, and immediately coughed. The smoke he inhaled the day before had left his throat raw and sore.

He walked over to the corner and looked on Saint Pierre Street toward the river. He had never been able to see the river from there before. He was surprised to find that he could see all the way to the water. All was gone, except for the blackened piles of embers. There was now several tents in place near the former houses.

He could see a wagon and some men beside it slowly making its way towards him. They appeared to be handing out packages and boxes of food.

"Is widow Tourneur somewheres here abouts?" a woman asked from behind him.

When he turned he saw a woman of color, tall and slender, of about twenty-five years of age, walking toward him from the street.

"Why yes, ma'am she is in that tent over there," he said.

"If you will please wait I will get her for you."

Just as he approached the tent widow Tourneur came out.

"This woman is looking for you," he said.

"Yes, what can I do for you?" widow Tourneur asked the lady.

"My name is Maria Bobe and I works for Maria Pauley," the woman said. "She said that she wanted me to find you and give you her compliments, and that she understands that this fire has left you in a position of great need. She would like to help you out at this time. She said for me to tell you that she has more than she needs and that if you need clothes such as dresses and other garments that she would like for you to come by today at your convenience."

The widow Tourneur stood there in silence, her face and arms frozen in place for a moment. Her eyes were glistening and watery with tears. Then she remembered her manners.

"Maria, please come sit down here," as she pointed to the tree stump in the grass.

"This is a very wonderful thing you and Maria are doing for me," she said. "I barely know the two of you and yet you came here today to help me. I am ashamed to say I have nothing to give you in return for your kindness."

"Oh, widow Tourneur, don't feel that you must do that," Maria said. "Mrs. Pauley feels that it is important to help those in need."

"I am so humbled by this act of your kindness. When I awoke this morning, I had no idea what I would do for clothes. Then you appeared," widow Tourneur said. "You have been Heaven sent."

"Please, I do not wish to appear impertinent, tell me before you go, how is it that you have such eloquent speech and manners?" widow Tourneur asked.

"Oh no, I don't mind," Maria answered. "It is quite simple you see, I am a pardo libre, free woman of color, and Mrs. Pauley taught me how to read and write at an early age and how to speak to people. She has been very kind to me all these years."

"Thank you very much, I will be indebted to you forever," widow Tourneur said.

"I must be goin' now and I will tell Mrs. Pauley you will be by there today," Maria said as she walked away.

"Santiago what are you doing?" widow Tourneur asked after she had turned to look at him.

"I am getting the horse and cart ready to take you to see Mrs. Pauley," he answered. "I could hear what you two were talking about so I thought that I might just go ahead and get ready."

"In that case I will get the others up and going. Mrs. Martine slept well and appears to feel better this morning," widow Tourneur said.

"While you are doing that I will take the horse over to Burns's horse lot and get her some grain and water," Santiago said.

"Okay, boys, time to get your clothes on," the widow said as she entered the tent.

"Are we going to get something to eat?" Philipe asked.

"I sure hope so, but I do not know when," she answered.

"Would you happen to have some quinine powder for this headache of mine?" Mrs. Martine asked.

"No, I don't, but we will try and find you some after we eat," the widow said as she walked out of the tent.

"I brought you some flour, rice, beans and some drinking water," the voice of a man said. It made Mrs. Martine stop abruptly.

"Why? Wha's the matter with you Maria Martine, cat got your tongue?" The man asked as he got down off of his horse.

"You're okay," his wife screamed running from the front of the tent followed by her son. They both threw themselves on him and she kissed him.

"Whoa, I'm all covered in soot and ashes," he said as he gently pushed her back an inch or two.

"I don't mind," she said. "The important thing is that you are still alive and back here with us."

"Yea, dad, how did you get all that stuff on you any way?" Jon asked.

"To begin with I helped some people get out of their house while it was burning. Then after that I worked with the soldiers while they pulled down some burned out houses in order to control the fire," he answered.

"Widow Tourneur and I will get started on fixing the food while you and Jon talk," Mrs. Martine said.

"Where is my brother?" Jon asked.

"He is with the neighbors," Jacques answered. "They got out early on before the fire got to this area and were able to save some of their chairs."

"Let's go to the tent and I can tell you some more while we sit. I am very tired," Jacques said to him.

As they walked to the tent, they saw Mrs. Martine and the widow getting the fire started. They had found a skillet and an old cooking pot in the ashes and cleaned them. Soon they were making biscuits and boiling the rice.

Santiago rode up in the cart.

"I could smell those biscuits a block away," he said.

"You are just in time Santiago. They will be ready shortly," the widow Tourneur said.

"Señor Santiago, I have some good news for you, Monsieur Jacques is here," Philipe said, in an excited voice.

"That is very good news," Santiago said, as he tied off his horse.

"He brought the food and water," Philipe explained.

"I am glad he did that. I am starved," Santiago said.

"Santiago, man am I glad to see you," Jacques said excitedly. "My wife has been telling me, just now, about how you went into our burning house and rescued her and my son."

"My family and I are deeply indebted to you for what you have done," Jacques said, in humble tone while shaking his hand.

"Thank you," Santiago answered. "But, to be truthful with you, I must confess, it almost did not happen. You see, when I first saw the fire I was gripped with fear and panicked. I jumped on my horse and ran away. After a few minutes I came to my senses and returned," Santiago explained, in a very meek voice.

Jacques said, "I am certainly glad that you did."

He put his hands on Santiago's shoulders and looking him squarely in the eyes said, "Always remember this, my friend, that without fear there can be no courage."

Santiago shook his head in agreement.

Jacques said, "Come on now, lets eat some of these biscuits and rice."

Santiago felt better about himself after this conversation and the meal. He was glad and relieved that he had told someone about what he had done. Also, he was glad to know, that his fears were no different from anyone else's, and that at the right time, he had done the right thing.

By the end of the day the army had provided tents provided for Philipe and Santiago and the neighbors. Some food also had been distributed by them. This made the whole situation more tolerable.

That afternoon he decided it would be a good time to take his horse back to Burns's for more water and grain.

He had been at the horse lot for almost an hour, when a familiar face came strolling up. It was his contact and fellow spy Diego Castellano.

"Hello Santiago, how have you been?" Diego asked in cheerful voice.

Santiago replied, "I am fine now, but I was worried about you. I did not see you for two days now. I was afraid you had died in the fire."

"Oh no, I was helping some people get their effects out of their houses," Diego said.

"That was very kind of you," Santiago stated.

"Why don't you meet with me tomorrow night at the bistro by the river and we can talk over our experiences from the last two days?" Diego asked.

Santiago answered, "I would like that very much."

"Okay Amigo, I see you then," Diego said, as he walked west on Dauphine Street.

Santiago was some what puzzled as he watched Diego walk away. He wondered why his clothes were clean and his face and hands had no sign of soot or dirt.

Then he thought, *Maybe he washed and changed clothes.* He dismissed that question as just suspicious nonsense. He put it out of his mind.

The events of the last two days left him emotionally and mentally fatigued and his mind began to focus on what brought to this place.

As he looked off toward the river, and over the devastation in between, the memory of how he arrived here began to dominate his thoughts.

Chapter 20

The time he spent in Newgate prison in London seemed like ages ago. He recalled one particular morning while he was soundly asleep, he had a dream about a girl back home. Margareta was her name, with red hair with dark brown eyes. He could feel the taste of her lips and the gentle caress of her soft hands on his neck and face.

Slowly he opened his eyes. There on his chest, by his hands, was a very large, black Norway rat. Its mouth was wide open and smelling of his face. There were two long front teeth protruding as though it were ready to bite anything in sight.

He immediately jumped to his feet and let out a very loud "AHHHAUGH" as he slammed the creature against the wall.

Falling to the floor, it lay there motionless for a moment. Then amazingly, the rat righted itself and crawled out under the door.

The whole time, two guards had been watching him through the opening in the door.

One of guards said, "Oh, Señor are you having fun dancing with the rats?"

In his anger, Santiago picked up his empty soup pail and flung it at the barred opening in the door and screamed at the top of lungs, "LET ME OUT OF HERE!"

He could hear the guards laughing while they walked away.

Then he heard a different kind of noise. A noise coming from the opposite direction. Coming from the cell next to his. A cell that, up until now, had been empty. So, this was the reason the guards had been there. Suddenly a quiet moaning came from the cell, sounded as though someone were in pain.

There was not a regular opening between the two cells. However, he had discovered some time ago a small hole in the wall. It was about the size of a piece a straw, like the ones in the mattress. He peeked through the hole and saw light on the other side. Then suddenly the light disappeared into darkness. He thought, *someone must have sat down and leaned against the other side of the hole.*

Should he say something to the new fellow? What if the guards put a spy in there? If he said something he may get a beating himself. He decided to take the chance anyway.

Santiago whispered, "Hola, amic" (*hello, friend*).

There was no answer. He thought, *Maybe he does not speak Catalan as I do. I shall try again in Spanish.*

Again, he whispered, "Hola, Amigo," (*hello, friend*).

Still, no answer. He felt his anxiety rising. In spite of this, he was over whelmed with curiosity. He had to know. Quickly he tore a small hole in the mattress and very carefully removed a long piece of straw. It was not too wide and it fit in the hole in the wall perfectly. Slowly he inserted the straw into the hole until it could go no further. There were a few inches protruding out on his side so he gave it a good hard shove.

Then he heard someone say, "Ouch, what th' heck?"

Santiago quickly removed the straw and looked in the hole. There was light. Then, an eyeball quickly appeared!

Again, he said, "Hola, Amigo,.."

The voice from the other side answered, "Hello, friend."

Santiago quickly answered, "From your words I can tell that you must be English."

The voice answered, "No, I am an American from Boston. My name is Joseph."

Santiago thought it strange that an American would be in an English prison. Maybe he was a spy. Then he thought, if I ask him some questions I can find out more.

"Joseph, how is it that you are here in this place?" Santiago asked.

Joseph answered, "I was a sailor on an American merchant ship bound for Jamica. It was the brig *Mary* out of Philadelphia. We were captured by a British man-o-war at about the half-way point."

After hearing, this Santiago began to feel more at ease.

Santiago asked, "Why did the British navy put you in jail?"

Joseph explained, "We, being myself and three other mates, were forced off our ship and into their hold. They put us in irons. It seems that they think we Americans do not have the right to carry out trade with other countries."

"My friend, let me tell you where you are. This is Newgate prison and it is a terrible place," Santiago said. "The guards are fat and lazy and the food is not fit for pigs to eat."

Joseph complained, "These leg irons are beginning to rub my ankles raw."

Santiago felt completely relieved at hearing this.

He said, "I am glad to hear that, my friend. I am saying that not to be cruel, but to let you know, that now I know you are not a spy. The guards would not put one of their own people in chains."

"I understand, my friend," Joseph replied.

Santiago asked, "How long do you have to keep them on?"

Joseph said, "I guess forever."

Santiago explained, "I have been here for about six months, I think. I had no identity papers. So, because of that I may be here for a very long time."

Joseph said in a depressed voice, "You and I, we are in a very bad way here in this place. From what you say it is a very old prison with a bad reputation."

Santiago said, "Let me tell you this, when I first got here I had some money. I could use that to pay the guards to give me some real food three times a day. They put me in a better cell with a window where I could see the court yard. The bed was soft and had a blanket."

Joseph laughed and said, "You must have thought you were in a fancy rooming house."

Santiago replied, "Yes, but then the money ran out and now here I am in this pit."

"What has it been like for you in this cell?" Joseph asked.

Santiago began, "I will tell you, there are three different kinds of cock roaches in here. The big ones, about the size of my thumb, can crawl up the wall, the ceiling and on the floor as well. The medium-sized ones, about half the size of the big ones, stay mainly on the floor in the corners. Then there are the small ones, half the size of the medium ones. They occasionally wander into the cell, from under the door, when the food is served."

"And you know what else?" Santiago asked.

"No, what is that?" Joseph asked.

"Due to the persistent presence of this variety of vermin, I am never in want for company at mealtime," Santiago exclaimed and then laughed.

Joseph replied, "I think I want to vomit."

Santiago said, "The food, if you want to call it that, consists mainly of cold potato soup, served in a metal pail. At first, I loathed the sight of the roaches, but as time went by, I slowly found a benefit to their existence. When the daily fare of soup, served up by the guard, was too thin, I would grab a few of the slower and fatter ones, mash them into the pail with the soup de jour. I prefer the larger ones because, after all, they add a little exotic flavor. Disgusting, yes, but I learned how to survive."

Joseph asked indignantly, "Surely you are joking with me, yes?"

Santiago described more, "you have not heard the worst part yet. If the roaches are not bad enough, then there are the rats. To begin with there were the small grey ones. Kind of cute I think and not very aggressive. They went after the roaches more than my food.

"But, slowly over time, they began to disappear until finally one day I noticed they were all gone. That was about the time the larger black Norway rats started to appear. I figured that the bigger black ones had eaten the smaller grey ones."

Chapter 21

Santiago and Joseph continued to talk to one another through the small hole in the wall between their cells.

"Have you ever tried to escape?" Joseph asked.

"Escape is impossible," Santiago answered, "The door or maybe that little window up there on the wall are the only ways out. But, even if you get out that door you still have to make it passed the guard who is a good sixty feet away. He would have plenty of time to grab his pistol and sabre."

Joseph moaned, "I think, I have a fever."

Santiago said, "You could ask the guards for some quinine powder."

The next morning the guards delivered the morning meal through the small opening in the bottom of the door and left as usual. Santiago quickly, with his pail in hand, moved to the opposite corner of his cell near the hole in the wall, out of sight from the little window in the door.

He whispered softly, "Hey, Amigo, how is your fever?"

"My fever has been with me about two days," Joseph replied, "And now it is causing these pus and scabs to grow around my ankles."

"Maybe this place has a doctor," Santiago suggested.

Joseph asked, "What could he do?"

Santiago answered, "Possibly a poultice."

"When I was on board ship the only time an officer would call the surgeon was when someone had died," Joseph replied. "Maybe it is worth a try. The worse he can do is put me out of my misery."

"The guards have started checking the cell four times a day," Santiago said. "Also today I noticed they have spiffy new uniforms with shiny buckles. I wonder what they are up to."

Santiago quickly said, "Quiet, listen I hear the footsteps of a guard coming down the hallway."

He scurried back to his bunk. Just then, the guard's face appeared in the upper window of the cell door. He appeared friendlier than usual.

The guard asked, "How are you today?"

"How fine can a person be in a place like this?" Santiago asked, with a somewhat indignant response.

He said, "Oh by the way is the fellow in the next cell sick or something?"

"I will check and see," the guard answered.

Santiago thought this was an unusually compassionate response. Curiosity got the best of him.

Santiago asked the guard as he started to walk away toward Joseph's cell, "Why the new uniform?"

The guard answered, "We have important visitors coming tomorrow."

This answer worried him. He remembered the last time there were important visitors. It was for an execution. He could barely hear the guard talking to Joseph through his cell door. He could hear their voices, but not loud enough to be understood. Soon the guard left.

Santiago returned to the hole in the wall and asked, "Amigo, what did the guard say about the surgeon?"

"He said he would ask. He also said the surgeon would come here soon and then be here for several days," Joseph said. "There are very many sick prisoners."

"This answer troubles me very much," Santiago said. "Why would the prison officials care so much now about the welfare of the prisoners? They never have in the past."

He said, "If they were going to have an execution, why would it matter if the prisoners are in a healthy condition?"

Joseph answered, "I think they are going to have the execution as you say, but that there will be high ranking royal guest here to witness it."

Santiago was silent for a moment then said, "Remember what I said about escape?"

"Yes," Joseph replied.

"I have changed my mind," Santiago said. "We should make plans for some kind of escape."

"I'm all for that," Joseph declared.

"But, can we do that without getting killed?" he asked in a high pitched voice.

"I will take some time to think this through. So don't go far away," Santiago said.

"Do not worry, my friend; I am locked up the same as you," Joseph replied, in a sarcastic laughing voice.

"I must return to my bunk to think," Santiago said.

About an hour later, he heard the guards walk passed his door, and stopped at Joseph's. Again, he could hear them talking, but he could not understand the words. He heard the door open and the sound of chains. Then the door closed. The guard walked passed his door without stopping. His imagination was starting to run wild about the things his friend was told. Was there talk of execution? He had to know. He immediately went back to the hole in the wall.

He asked, "Amigo, I have to know. What did they say?"

Joseph answered, "They said only that the surgeon wanted my chains removed."

"That was it? That was all?" Santiago asked excitedly.

"Yes," Joseph answered.

"If this means what I think it means then we should most definitely plan that escape," Santiago said.

"I agree," Joseph said, "I think I am marked for execution."

Santiago declared, in a strained voice, "Amigo, my heart sinks for you. If it is true then I will surely be next."

Chapter 22

Santiago said, "Now I will tell you my plan for escape. When they deliver breakfast tomorrow morning to my door I will be lying on the floor acting like I'm in pain. I will tell the guard I have fallen and ask him to come inside and help me get up. When he comes in and bends over to help me, I will hit him on the head with a piece of wood from the bed post. I will then grab his keys and let you out. We will then make our way down the hall to his station, get his gun and sabre. At this time of day, all the other guards are either busy in their units or eating in the dining hall.

At that point, we can make it down the stairs, out the door, across the courtyard and through the front gate in a matter of minutes. Then we get two horses from the remuda outside the gate and we are on our way."

"That plan sounds as good as any," Joseph says.

Santiago looked up toward the window in the wall and he saw that the sun had already set. Then there is the usual knock on his door signaling that his evening bowl of potato soup has arrived once more.

The next morning arrived early. The sun was not up yet, but Santiago very quietly slipped out of his bunk. In the dark, he slowly loosened one of the heavy pieces of wood holding the foot end of the bed in place. It was about two feet long. He was able to lean the bed against the wall so it would not fall down.

He carefully laid the piece of wood under the head of the bed out of site through the little window in the door.

By his reckoning, it would probably be about one hour before the guard will deliver the breakfast. He crept quietly to the hole in the wall.

He whispered, "Amigo, wakeup."

Joseph whispered back, "I am awake."

"Are you ready?" Santiago asked.

"Yes, I am ready," Joseph answered.

Time went by very slowly while they are waiting. Santiago cursed the day he entered into this place. His was tired of waiting. He wanted to get it over with. Then he heard boot steps.

"They are coming, get ready," Santiago said.

Santiago positions himself near the head of the bed.

He begins to moan loudly, "Oh, help me I have fallen!"

He repeats this several times. Then the boots stopped at the door. He heard the jingling of keys. He griped the wood tightly. The door opened and Santiago saw the guard. He was dressed in a bright, red, new uniform with clean white leggings. The guard quickly steps in. Santiago looks up and can see into the hallway passed the guard. There were three other men in the hallway, two more guards and the Captain of the Guard. They too were wearing new uniforms.

The guard said, "Let me help you up, old chap."

Santiago was stunned. He did not know what to think. Suddenly he realized that an attempt at escape would be futile. He thought this must be some kind of special execution squad.

The Captain of the Guard said in a loud, voice, "Santiago De Barcelona, come out of your cell!"

Santiago stood up and said, "Yes, sir."

He walked into the hallway and stopped about a foot in front of the Captain.

The Captain immediately pulled his head back and asked, "How long has it been since this chap has had a bath?"

The second corporal answered, "Judging by the smell, I would say about six months sir."

"He also appears to have lice and no telling what other kind of vermin in his hair," the captain added.

"Bring out that other fellow in the next cell as well," the captain said.

Turning to the first corporal, the captain commanded in a loud English accent, "Take these two to the infirmary and have the surgeon treat their hair."

He looked at Santiago again and pointed to him with his quirt and said, "As well have them do something about those sores on this chap's face."

Off they went down the hallway with the captain leading the way followed by the first corporal, Santiago and Joseph shoulder to shoulder, the second corporal and the Private behind them. They went down the stairs and out the lower floor door.

Santiago asked Joseph, "You want to know what I think?"

"Sure, tell me," Joseph answered.

"They are going to a hell of a lot of trouble for an execution. There would be no reason to clean us up just to hang us," Santiago said

Santiago looked at the waist bands on the guards.

"Joseph look at the guards, do you see what I see?" he asked.

"They have their sabers, but no rifles or pistols," Joseph answered.

Santiago thinking out loud, said, "Maybe this is not an execution after all."

Chapter 23

The two prisoners looked at each other bewildered. The guards paid little attention to their conversation. They reached the infirmary and entered through the narrow door.

The captain had the guards stand at ease and addressed the two prisoners.

"This is the luckiest day of your lives," he began, "We have a special assignment for the two of you. If you survive this ordeal your sentence will be commuted and you will be set free."

Both prisoners smiled.

They both asked simultaneously, "What do we have to do?"

The captain answered, "It's quite simple, you will be inoculated with cowpox. And if you live afterwards you will become free men. What do you say fellas, you two chaps want to give it a go?"

Santiago looked at Joseph and nodded.

Santiago said, "Yes, anything is better than dying."

"Jolly good shew, men," he exclaimed.

At that point, the surgeon entered the room and examined them both. He put some alcohol-coal tar smelling stuff on Santiago's hair and treated his facial sores with a similar smelling, gooey looking salve.

The surgeon then said, "In about an hour wipe this stuff off of them and proceed with the bathing."

They sat in the room for exactly one hour. One of the guards came in, had them stand up and cleaned their faces and hair.

The guard turned to the first corporal and nodded. The first corporal commanded, "Proceed with giving them a bath. When you have finished come and let me know."

The guard clicked his heels together and answered, "Yes, Corporal."

Santiago and Joseph went into a small room. In there was a metal bathtub big enough for only one person.

The corporal said, "One of you take the bucket, go to the kitchen in the next building and tell the cook to give you some hot water for the bath. Over there on the table is the soap and some towels. I will be back shortly with some clean clothes."

Santiago turned to Joseph and said quickly, "Here is the soap so why don't you get ready to take the first bath and I will go get you some hot water?"

Joseph answered, "Oh I know what you are up to. You want to go over to the kitchen and see if there is a pretty little cook in there."

Santiago said, "Why, Joseph, I am so interested in getting out of here that I cannot even think about women."

Joseph replied, "Oh, don't give me that hog wash. I know what you want to do. You want to find one and keep her all to yourself."

Santiago grabbed a towel and tossed it over Joseph's head and said, "You better hurry up and get in that bath. If you don't, those Brits may come back in here and change their minds."

Santiago made his way over next door to the kitchen where the door was open; there he saw one of the cooks inside chopping onions for the officers' supper.

He stood in the doorway and said through the door, "It has been so long since I have smelled fresh onions, it is wonderful. Can I get a bucket of hot water for the bath next door?"

Maria, the cook, looked up and saw Santiago standing there. She paused for a few seconds to gaze into his handsome face.

"Yes, of course help yourself," she said.

Her eyes were fixed on his manly facial features, especially his dark hair and eyes. She instantly noticed the heavy eyebrows that came together on his forehead. The odor of onions was very heavy in the tiny kitchen so that it masked the odor of his body.

She said, "Here, hand me your bucket and I will dip up the water for you."

"Thank you very much," he answered, smiling.

After she filled the bucket, she walked over to him. When she drew close enough to him to hand him the bucket, she realized why he had to take a bath. She immediately stepped back a couple of paces.

"What did they make you do, sleep in a pig pen?" she asked.

"Oh no, nothing like that, just with the rats and roaches," Santiago answered.

"Here, I have this bottle of lilac water. Please take and sprinkle it on yourself after the bath," she suggested.

"Oh, thank you so very much. I will share it with my friend Joseph, he will certainly need it also," Santiago replied.

"That will be fine with me. Use the whole bottle if you need too," she said.

Santiago took the bucket of water and walked away, he abruptly stopped.

"Maybe I will see you later?" he asked.

"It is possible, if you are lucky," she quipped.

As he walked away, she stood in the doorway with her arms crossed. She could not help admire his tight prison pants, as he disappeared into the infirmary.

When he arrived in the infirmary he realized there was not enough water in the tub.

"Joseph, I do not think this one bucket will be enough for me. While I am getting into the tub can you go to the kitchen and get another bucket of water?" Santiago asked.

"Oh yea sure, no problem," Joseph answered.

When Joseph arrived in the kitchen, he saw Maria there.

"Hi, my name is Joseph and you must be the cook," he said.

She answered smiling, "Yes, my name is Maria. Are you Santiago's friend?"

"Yes," Joseph answered.

"Do you feel better after your bath?" Maria asked.

"Like a new man," Joseph explained. "Santiago is taking his bath now and needs some more hot water."

"Oh, really, then I will take the bucket to him," she said, and grabbed the bucket from Joseph.

"Okay then, I will go out into the court yard and smoke this pipe," Joseph said.

After Joseph left, Maria filled the bucket, grabbed a bar of lilac soap and headed for the infirmary. She quietly entered the room where Santiago was in the tub. He was facing the opposite direction from her. He heard the door close.

"Joseph, pour the water in now it is starting to get cold in this tub," Santiago said.

Maria quietly walked up behind the tub. She gently poured the hot water over his shoulder.

He began to speak, "Joseph, thank you…"

When he smelled the odor of onions he stopped speaking abruptly, then turned his head.

"Oh hello, you are not Joseph," he said, with a smile.

"I thought you might like some help with your bath," she replied.

She rubbed the wet bar of lilac soap on his shoulders.

"The captain likes for me to help him with his bath," Maria said.

"I see, what about the other men here, do you help them with baths also?" Santiago asked.

"Oh no, just the captain, he has given me strict instructions never to do that for any of the other soldiers," she answered.

"Are you his woman?" Santiago inquired.

"Sort of, kind of," she answered.

She had her arms deep in the soapy water, washing the lower part of his sides and back.

"That feels so good. I have not had a bath since I was put in that cell," Santiago said, while laying his head back.

Maria smiled and continued her slow rhythmic washing motion. Just then, there was a knock on the door.

"This is the captain and I have some papers for you," the man said.

At that same moment, he opened the door. Also at that same moment, Maria could not possibly get out the back door. She squatted down behind the tub.

"Okay, but as you can see I am still in the tub. Can you put them on the table?" Santiago asked.

"These are requisitions for your clothes. Since you are a civilian you must sign for them," the captain explained.

He placed them on the table that was across the room from the tub. He started out the door. At that time, Maria began to raise up her head. The captain stopped abruptly and turned back. Santiago reached over the side of the tub with his right arm, and without moving his head, gently put his hand on Maria's head and pushed it down.

"Be sure to have the other fellow sign them also," the Captain said.

"Yes, of course," Santiago answered.

The captain turned and put his hand on the handle and began to step out the door. Maria slowly raised her head.

"Oh, by the way," the captain said. "If the clothes do not fit just, let me know and we can find some more."

Again, Santiago pushed Maria's head down gently, out of sight. Finally, the captain turned and left, pulling the door closed behind him.

"That was close," Maria stated, as she stood up quickly.

"I think it is time for you to go before we both get into a lot of trouble," Santiago said, standing up and putting the towel around his waist.

Smiling she gave him a little squeeze on the right shoulder and slipped out the back very quickly. She stopped in the doorway and quickly turned around for one last look at him and the thick, black, burly hair on his chest.

Chapter 24

Shortly thereafter Joseph returned. As he entered the door, he encountered Santiago.

"Amigo, this is very good tobacco, it is smooth and does not bite. The corporal said it came from New Orleans."

"Oh really, I will have to try some. How do your clothes fit?" Santiago asked.

"See the pants are nice looking, but kind of big," Joseph answered laughingly.

He held out the waistband of his pants to show the gap.

"The Captain said if they do not fit to see him and he will get some that do," Santiago said.

"I will do that shortly," Joseph said.

"Pass me some of that tobacco. I want to try it in this pipe the corporal gave me," Santiago said with a smile.

After he lit the pipe, he drew in a few puffs and slowly blew out the smoke.

"You say this came from New Orleans? It just so happens that I have a cousin there," Santiago said, while beaming with a smile.

"He is a priest. Can you imagine that, a fellow like me with priest for a cousin?" Santiago asked.

"What is his name?" Joseph asked.

Santiago replied, "It is Fr. Tomas de Rodrigo."

"He is a few years older than me and much more righteous," he said with a slight laugh. "He taught me how to read and write when I was just a boy. He was a priest even then."

"I can tell you admired him very much," Joseph said.

"Oh yes," Santiago answered. "He was the pride of the whole family. Before he left for Spanish Louisiana he gave me some advice. He said 'Santiago you are very smart, but you have a penchant for wild ideas and you must guard yourself against them. They will always bring you trouble'."

Joseph said, "That is good advice for any man."

Santiago said, in a low sad voice, "I want to go there and see him some day."

"I'm sure you will," Joseph said.

"Enough of this melancholy, I feel like dancing," Santiago said, as he jumped to his feet.

He stepped into the middle of the floor and took the stance of a Flamingo dancer. He began to snap his fingers above his head and tap his heels on the floor in a Flamingo rhythm.

As he did this, he began to say, "Today is a great day. This morning I was a prisoner in a cell. Now I will be free. I had a bath, new clothes, a shave and a pretty girl. What more can a man wish for?" he asked, while he continued to dance in a slow circle.

Joseph said with a big smile, "Man you are wild and crazy."

Finally, Santiago stopped and said, "Let us go and see if the supper is ready, I'm starved and I bet you are too."

The meals that they were given were not the usual potato soup, but the same that the guards ate. Later they were placed in an empty barracks. This night when they went to sleep, they did not feel the usual anxiety. This was the first pleasant night sleep Santiago had in several months.

Chapter 25

The next morning after waking up, he noticed Joseph was still sound asleep.

Santiago said, "Hey, Amigo, it is time to get up. Today is the big day for us."

"This was the best mattress. I have not slept on one like this since Boston. I'm not dreaming, am I?" Joseph asked.

"No, my friend, it is really happening," Santiago answered.

After Santiago put his shirt on, he looked out the window.

"Come and look at this, I see one heck of a fancy carriage," Santiago said.

Joseph jumped up out bed and looked out the window.

"Wow, man, I have not seen one like that since I was in Madrid. Do you think the guests are some of the royal family?" Santiago asked, in a loud voice.

"Let's get dressed and go to chow. Maybe someone there knows what is going on?" Joseph asked.

"Good idea," Santiago replied.

As they entered the mess hall, they stopped just inside the door.

"Look at all these soldiers. They are not the regular guards," Santiago said.

"They must have come in with that carriage," Joseph stated.

"We should sit over there," Santiago said, pointing to a table in the corner across the room.

While getting their food they talked to one of the cooks.

"We noticed the fancy carriage out in the court yard. Did the soldiers arrive with it?" Santiago asked.

"Yes, late last night, the captain got me out of bed to fix the people and the soldiers a late supper," the cook explained.

"Are they an escort for some royalty?" Joseph asked.

"The group is the Duchess of Willingham and her sister, along with their Ladies in Waiting. They are here for some special meeting with a surgeon from the Admiralty in London," the cook answered.

"That means us!" Santiago and Joseph exclaimed simultaneously.

The two of them hurriedly ate then left and headed for the barracks. While on their way, they met up with the Captain of the Guard.

"I say, good morning, fellas, I'm glad I came upon you this way, I was just coming over to collect you for our meeting. If you are ready we can go to my office straight away?" The captain asked.

"Yes, sir, we are ready," Santiago answered.

The captain asked as they walked, "I trust you men had a good nights sleep?"

"Oh yes we did, sir, very well indeed," Santiago answered.

They reached the main building and went up stairs to the captain's office. When they entered the room, they found it half full of people.

Seated along the wall by the window were the Duchess, her sister, their two ladies, the surgeon and an army major.

On the other side of the room was a small table with a chair on each side. The top was covered with a cloth. On top of that were several small glass bottles with liquid in them and some rather large looking toothpicks sitting about on the cloth.

"Santiago and Joseph, if you please, have a seat by the table," the Captain of the Guard said.

Santiago was not quite sure what was about to happen. He felt perspiration build under his arms. Just then, the Captain of the Guard stepped out from behind his desk.

"We are gathered here today to conduct an experiment with a new type of smallpox vaccine," he said.

Santiago settled in for a boring speech. He had formed the opinion, from prior experiences, that this captain was enchanted with the sound of his own voice. The room smelled heavily of perfume. The cheap kind that he would expect to be found on a lady of the evening.

"This formulation, as it is called, is made from the pustules of a cow with cowpox, a disease similar to smallpox in humans," he said. "It has been shown that when this formulation is injected under the skin of humans it will produce immunity to that disease."

At this point all the ladies took out their hankies and held them up to their noses.

The Captain of the Guard carried on in great oratory fashion, as he was now standing in front of the ladies. With his walking back and forth, his head pushed high, and leaning slightly back, he appeared as though he were a peacock strutting in front of a bunch of hens. Santiago found it difficult to hide the sense of amusement on his face.

"We have the great honor to have present here today, to witness this procedure, as representatives of the Royal family, The Duchess of Willingham, her sister and their ladies. The Royal family, it seems, has a keen interest in a faster and better method for inoculation against smallpox. They have heard of the cowpox approach and would like to see it tested," the captain explained.

While this was being said, Santiago was looking at the Duchess and her at him. She had found his manly features very appealing. Their eyes met. She held that gaze for several seconds. Realizing this, she quickly turned her head to the right. She looked to her lady who also looked at her. The expression on her lady's face seemed to say, 'I see what you are doing'.

She turned her eyes back towards him as if to see if he was still looking at her. She saw his eyes fixed upon her. Her pulse began to go faster and her hands became moist with perspiration.

"And now the surgeon will proceed with the inoculation," the captain announced.

"Oh, I see it is almost ten in the morning. Let us stop now for a spot of tea," the captain said, after he looked at his watch.

"Sergeant, go and fetch us tea all around," he ordered. The sergeant immediately left the room.

Chapter 26

Shortly thereafter, the sergeant returned with the assistance of
Maria. Immediately upon entering the room, she saw Santiago
and momentarily fixed her eyes upon him. Then remembering
what she was supposed to be doing she turned her head and
paid attention to her duties.

She was carrying a very large, shiny, silver serving tray holding nine
cups and saucers in the Strawberry Fair design; as well as a large tea
pot, small creamer, sugar bowl and teaspoons, all in sterling silver. This
made the tray very heavy and the strain on her face was obvious.

Beginning with the Duchess, Maria and the sergeant served each
person a cup of hot tea.

Finally, they finished serving everyone including Santiago and
Joseph. At that time, Maria left the room. For the next half hour, the
people in the room made polite conversation. Then Maria returned and
collected all the cups and saucers on the silver platter.

The Captain of the Guard again stood up and clearing his throat said, "I think that after that splendid tea we should continue on with the inoculation. Doctor, if you please."

"If you would be so kind, sir, will you please roll up your sleeve?" the surgeon asked, as he approached Santiago.

He was surprised at the surgeon's polite manner and speech, "Yes, sir, of course," Santiago answered.

Santiago watched intently at what the surgeon was doing. He dipped one of the small sticks into the formulation.

"Now my boy, you will feel a little stick on the skin," he warned, as he jabbed him with the stick.

"Oh, that wasn't so bad," Santiago said, after jumping slightly in his chair.

The surgeon then inoculated Joseph in the same way.

"The site of the inoculation may become red and swollen. That will only be temporary. In a few days you may feel a fever or maybe not. If you do come down with a fever, do not be alarmed, for it will pass in a day or so. In a fortnight, you will be challenged by another kind of dose. It will be from a patient who presently has smallpox. At that point you should not show any signs of a reaction, proving you are protected against the disease," the surgeon explained.

"When that is all done, both of you will be free to go," the Captain of the Guard said.

Two weeks later all went well, including the challenge dose. Santiago really was a free man now. Or so he thought.

While sitting on his bunk he began to ponder *where will I go and what will I do?* Then a realization began to sink in on him. He and Joseph were both in the same predicament. Just about that time Joseph came in.

"Mate, you look like you have been doing some heavy thinking!" Joseph exclaimed.

"You are right, mi Amigo. It has just dawned on me. We are free are we not? You better think again. We are not free. We are in a financial bind. We have no clothes except what is on our backs. We have no horse and no money for traveling. We are very much stuck. What are we going to do?" Santiago asked.

"We certainly do not want to stay around here. This place gives me the creeps," Joseph replied.

"I agree," replied Santiago.

"You know, come to think of it, that Captain of the Guard has been very nice to us," Santiago said. "I just wonder if he might know of a way we could earn some money in a short period of time?"

"Maybe," Joseph replied.

"Would you like to go with me to ask him?" Santiago asked.

"Oh yes, sir!" Joseph exclaimed with a big grin on his face.

At that point, both of them jumped up and headed out the door and across the courtyard. They quickly went up the stairs. But, then they were stopped. There on each side of the door to the Captain's office were guards with muskets and bayonets.

"Halt!" yelled one of the guards, while putting out his hand.

"We would like to see the captain, if at all possible?" Santiago asked, almost breathlessly.

"He has another officer in there and cannot be disturbed," the guard said.-

"Oh I see," said Santiago.

"You two may sit at the end of the hall in those chairs," the guard instructed them.

"I wonder how long we will have to wait?" Joseph asked Santiago.

"Seeing what our situation is, I will wait all night if I have too," Santiago replied.

They did not have to wait very long.

Santiago pointed in the guards' direction and said, "Look someone is coming out the door. Let's go there now," Joseph said.

As they approached, they were able to see the officer coming out of the doorway.

"Look it is that army major who was present during our inoculation two weeks ago," Santiago said.

"I wonder why he would be back here?" Joseph asked.

At that point, one of the guards said, "You may go in now."

"Please come in and tell me how may I help you?" the captain asked as they walked in.

"Sir, you see we were planning on leaving today, but then we realized that we had no money, no clothes and no horse," Santiago began.

"Can you help us find some work here so we could save some money?" Joseph asked.

While Joseph was speaking, the captain was nodding.

"I think I can help you," he answered.

Santiago and Joseph looked at each other with big smiles.

"It seems that we have had a couple of stable boys that took off, for who knows where, two days ago. So we are in need of help in that area. I am afraid that is all we have here at the moment. Would you be interested in that?" The captain asked, in an apologetic tone.

At hearing that news, their faces turned from smiles to gloom, but said in unison, "Okay."

"Jolly good shew, then that is all settled. You chaps will start tomorrow morning," he stated, in a joyful tone.

Santiago and Joseph quickly said, "Yes, sir."

They left the office and made their way to the mess hall of the guards. After they arrived there, a guard that they recognized, came up to them and took Santiago aside by the arm.

"Ol' chap, the captain would like to have a word with you, now," he commanded.

Chapter 27

Santiago and the guard left the mess hall while Joseph stayed behind at a table.

In the office the captain gestured towards a chair and said to Santiago, "Please be seated."

The captain said, "I appreciate that you are taking time from your meal for this meeting. I think that you noticed before our meeting earlier this afternoon that I had a visitor just ahead of you. His visit was somewhat unexpected. I think that you may be interested in what he and I discussed. His name is Pullman and he is quite heavily involved with reconnaissance of territories outside of the British Empire. This activity requires the collecting of geographical information for the making of maps and that sort of thing. At the present time he is in need of someone who is a former military type and of Spanish heritage. Someone who speaks the language fluently and is well acquainted with the customs."

The captain stood up out of his chair and leaned on the desk top with both hands in order to make a point.

"The position pays quite handsomely. This kind of money would be equal to that of an experienced army officer," the captain said.

This caught Santiago totally by surprise.

"Without going any further, do you think you would be interested?" the captain asked.

"Yes, of course," Santiago answered quickly.

"Splendid, now let us continue on," the captain said, with a smile.

"Major Pullman will fill you in on the greater details later," he said.

Santiago asked, "Will I wear a uniform?"

The captain answered, "Maybe, but I doubt it. This whole affair will be quite clandestine you see. Very hush hush and all that sort of thing. Pullman used the term undercover agent."

"Oh you mean spy," Santiago said bluntly.

"Yes, of course. As I'm sure you might suspect, there will be an element of danger involved. How is your experience with the sabre, pistol and musket?"

"It has been a few months, but still good I think," Santiago answered.

"Splendid, in the morning report back here to me. At that time we will arrange for your provisions, give you traveling money, a clothing allowance and further instructions," the captain said.

"Yes, sir," Santiago replied.

"Oh, one other thing, you must conduct yourself with complete secrecy. No one must know how you are involved. That includes your friend Joseph."

At that point, there was a knock on the door.

"Enter," the captain said.

The guard came in and the captain walked over and stood close by him as he whispered something into the captain's ear.

"Very well then," the captain said to the guard.

The guard turned about face and left the room and the captain walked up to Santiago.

"I must tell you that, for security reasons, you will not see your friend Joseph again. There is no reason to be concerned about him, for you see, as we speak, he is on his way to Liverpool. There he will board a ship that will take him to Philadelphia. He will have plenty of money and a comfortable cabin. When he arrives there, in about six weeks, he should not have any trouble finding a job as an ordinary seaman. Do you have any questions?" the captain asked.

"I do not know what to think," Santiago answered.

"When you return in the morning I am sure that Major Pullman can fill you in further," the captain explained.

Santiago had the feeling that the captain was trying to hurry him along and get him out of the office. He bid the captain good night and left. He immediately went to the mess hall where he ate steak and beans. He ate it with gusto, and the whole time he thought, *this may be my last good meal for a while.*

Chapter 28

The next morning after breakfast, a guard came to Santiago's barracks.

"I have come to collect you and escort you to the meeting with Major Pullman," he said.

It was strange, he thought, that the guard had neither pistol nor musket, only a saber. He was taken to the office of the Captain of the Guard. There he found the major sitting at the captain's desk.

"Shut the door and sit down. The captain is out today so I will be using his office for this meeting," Pullman said, sharply.

"You will find my methods different from those of the captain. I tend to move events along at a quicker pace," he explained quickly.

"Yes, sir, I see," Santiago answered.

"Here is some background on your assignment," he began in an authoritarian voice. "Back in 1779-1781, the Spanish General Galvez drove the English army out of that area known as the Florida West Parishes," he said, while pointing to a map on the wall.

He said, "You may also hear them referred to as Florida Occidental. The two most populated towns there, in addition to New Orleans, are Mobile and Pensacola. We need to have a man of ours in New Orleans, to help us keep track of the Spanish forces there. That person should be preferably of Spanish decent."

He paused for a few seconds then leaned forward in the chair and said, "Someone like you."

After a moment he said, "Also I should be honest and tell you that you will not be the first operative we have sent over there."

"May I ask happened to the others?" Santiago queried.

Pullman said, with a somber expression on his face, "Each one seemed to mysteriously disappear. I suspect that they failed to obey orders and were discovered, then executed. I expect you to succeed.

"Yes sir, Santiago said.

"In order to do that you must obey my orders and do exactly what I tell you to do. Is that understood?" he asked Santiago.

"Sir, I was a member of an elite Catalonian regiment and I welcome this kind of assignment," he answered, in a bragging tone.

"Oh really now," Pullman responded.

The major very calmly opened his valise and took out a folded document. Santiago could see the yellowish-brown colored papers. They had an official stamp of some kind on the back. He began to feel a little nervous, wondering what it was.

"Actually, Santiago, we have a complete dossier on you. It says here your father died when you were a teenager, raised by your mother, you had six brothers and two sisters and your mother had to take in washing from the neighbors to keep food on the table. Also at that time, you became a street brawler. There is something here about you violating a social code by visiting the neighborhood girls without a chaperon. Then you were under the supervision of a priest, by the name of Father Tomas, for skipping classes at the Catholic school. Next, there is an incident with the mayor's daughter, another social disgrace.

Lastly, when you were old enough you joined the Catalonian Regiment. You left that unit under questionable circumstances."

"Yes, sir, that is all correct," Santiago answered, while sitting and staring straight ahead.

After hearing this, he thought for sure that he would be put back in prison.

Pullman said loudly, "If you want to remain out of an English prison you will drop that arrogant part of your character and obey all my commands."

"Yes, sir, you can count on me," Santiago answered quickly.

Then Santiago abruptly left the room. The next thought that went through his mind was, *What have I gotten myself into now?*

Chapter 29

He heard a voice saying, "Santiago, Santiago". It was Philipe tugging at his sleeve and calling his name.

"It is almost sundown and I have been looking for you everywhere," Philipe said excitedly.

"Yes my young friend, it is time to go back," Santiago said, "My horse has had enough grain and water so let's go."

On their walk back down the road, Santiago thought about how interesting it will be to talk with Diego again at the tavern. Maybe then, he can find out what Diego did during the fire. It was curious that he did not see Diego during the fire. That will definitely be something for him to explain.

The next night, just after the sun had gone down, Santiago was walking into the entrance of the bistro when two well dressed men came out. They were busy talking to each other and paid no attention to him. He recognized one of them as Governor Miro. The other man he did not know.

After he went inside, he spotted Diego sitting at a corner table.

"Ah, Diego, you have gotten us a good table," he said.

"Please, my friend sit down and have some of this good wine," Diego replied. "We are lucky it survived the fire in good condition."

"Roseta, bring me a glass for the wine," Santiago yelled. "I am ready to cut loose tonight."

"So, tell me, where you were during the fire?" Santiago asked, "I did not see you in that mess."

"I tell you, I was with this, how I should say, 'Lady' the night before and I overslept," Diego said in a sly voice. "Remember when we were at that other tavern further down the quay that night and I introduced you to Rosey."

"Now I remember," Santiago said laughingly. "Oh yes, how I remember. My head hurts just to think of that night."

"I also overslept and I did not get out of bed until after the fire had started," Santiago said. "Philipe woke me up just about the time of the first explosion. Then we had to run for our lives."

"The last time I saw Rosey she was running up the River Road during the fire," Diego said.

"Oh really, where does she live?" Santiago asked.

"I do not know for sure, I think somewhere up there near the old Jesuit plantation," he answered.

Then Diego quickly changed the subject and said, "You should have been here earlier this evening. The governor was in here with one of his buddies."

"Yes, I saw them as I was coming in, who was that fellow?"

"He, my friend, was the one and only Jerome Pound," Diego answered with a big grinning smile.

"That name means nothing to me," Santiago responded, with curiosity.

"He is a very savvy, well healed Irishman who has been around in places like Philadelphia and Havana. He has friends that know every smuggler along the Mississippi River from here to the mouth of the Ohio," Diego explained.

"That is very impressive," Santiago said as he slowly sipped his wine.

"With his influence and connections he is not someone to be crossed," Diego replied.

"Is this someone who could be useful to us and our cause?" Santiago asked.

"Yes, most definitely, but in a very clandestine manner," Diego said, as leaned forward and squinted his eyes.

"Tell me more about him," Santiago inquired.

"The word I get is this, Pound first appeared in this city when O'Reilly was governor. It was that official who allowed him to operate openly with many trading privileges. When Unzaga took over from O'Reilly, Pound had developed some kind of a working relationship with the American government. However, it was later, under Galvez, that his smuggling activities bloomed, Diego explained."

"Did he ever work with the American rebels?" Santiago inquired.

"Yes," Diego answered, as he looked around the room to see if anyone was listening to their conversation. Then leaned closer to Santiago.

"Sometime around 1779 or 1780, the American rebels were making a push to move the British out of the western part of the Allegheny Mountains in the western part of Virginia. Pound setup a network of smugglers from the port of New Orleans all the way up the river to the area north of Natchez, and then east to the rebel forces," Diego said, in a hushed voice.

"What were they smuggling?" Santiago asked.

"A little bit of everything, but primarily gunpowder, medical supplies and money," Diego said.

"Money, wow," Santiago exclaimed quietly.

This time when Diego looked around the room, he spotted three Spanish officers from the Louisiana Infantry Regiment walking into the bistro. They seated themselves at a table in the middle of the room near the door.

He turned to Santiago and touched him on his left wrist to get his attention while he was just taking a sip of wine. Santiago looked toward him with curiosity on his face. At that moment, Diego cut his eyes to his left at the same time tilting his head. Then Diego put his finger up to his lips warning Santiago not to speak. Simultaneously both of them slowly stood from their chairs and the table.

They walked to the door and when they were close to the officer's table Diego said, "My friend I am sure I can find you another place to live, possibly on Royale Street near Urseline."

Santiago thought that this statement was a little odd. That area of the city was inhabited by very wealthy people. Maybe Diego intended that the officers hear that statement. If they did, they may think that he was a wealthy newcomer to the city.

At that point, the two of them walked through the door. One of the officers watched them as they went out. He took a pencil and a piece of paper out of his vest pocket and proceeded to write something on it.

They talked quietly as they walked toward their horses.

"Did you see those pistols they had in their belts?" Diego asked Santiago.

"Yes, I did," he answered. "What does that mean to you?"

"These Spanish officers would never carry their pistols if they were off duty. Neither would they go into a bistro while on duty," he answered.

He continued, "The only thing I can figure is, there must be some kind of an alert. But, why I do not know."

"Possibly something to do with the fire?" Santiago inquired.

"It could be," answered Diego. "The government here has a history of being very tight lipped about these things, so we may never know."

After they mounted their horses, they rode to the corner.

"I am going this way," Diego said, pointing toward the river bank. "Meet here again tomorrow night."

As he rode away along the river he noticed at the shoreline there were three ships anchored close together. They had not been there the day before. One of them was the *Governor Miro,* a schooner he had seen previously on the day he arrived. All three appeared to be riding high on the water as though they were empty of cargo. Seeing them peeked his curiosity and he thought *this would be a very good question for Diego.*

He thought about the conversation that evening and how Diego changed the subject and never answered the question about where he was during the fire. He must be hiding something about what he did during that time.

Chapter 30

On the way back to the tent he let the reins go slack so now the horse walked at a very slow pace. At the intersection of St. Philippe and Bourbon, he started to turn right toward Burns's but stopped. A movement further down St. Philippe at Dauphine caught his eye. It was two army officers on horseback carrying lanterns and riding their horses slowly.

"Wait up Señor, where are you headed tonight?" one of them asked.

"I am headed over here to Burns's to board my horse for the night," Santiago answered.

Santiago noticed that both of the men had pistols in their belts. This made him uneasy.

The officers said something to each other barely above a whisper.

Then they looked at Santiago and one of them said, "You have a good evening."

They turned and continued on St. Philippe Street. Santiago was not quite sure what to make of all that. Maybe they were only patrolling the city to prevent looters. He continued toward the lot and put up his horse.

There was an attendant there now who helped him with his saddle and accepted his payment. He was an older man and when he held out his hand for the payment Santiago pressed a gold Mexican centavo into his palm. The man held up a lantern beside his hand and looked at the coin.

He looked at Santiago with a smile and said, "Gracias señor."

As Santiago walked back to his tent he thought *How nice it would be to being lying on his own bed in his own bedroom and his head on a soft pillow. Maybe Diego was serious about finding him another place to live.*

Off in the distance, in the trees to his right, he could hear noises like drums beating and people singing. The closer he could see several fires burning all arranged to make a crude circle. Within that circle, there was another circle, made up of what appeared to be slaves. Inside that circle there was a woman standing alone and quiet. Now he was close enough to hear the chanting clearly. It was a language he did not recognize or had ever heard before.

The two officers on horseback he had seen earlier were there also, watching from the road. They were just beyond the trees. From their position they could see everything the people were doing.

He was finally close to his tent. He noticed that one of the officers was watching him very closely. He was not quite sure what to make of this. He decided to ask the widow tomorrow, certainly she would know. After all, she has been here for many years and knew much about the customs of the various nationalities.

Chapter 31

The next morning they all were around the fire between the tents. Santiago described to the widow what he had seen in the trees night before.

"They were all in a circle around a young woman. All the while chanting to the rhythm of those drums," he said.

"What was that all about?" Philipe asked.

Widow Tourneur answered, "They were the Caribbean slaves talking to the spirits so their people will be protected from any more fire, it is called Voudou."

"You mean the black magic?" Santiago asked.

"They believe in those spirits of theirs. They also go to the Catholic Church every Sunday," she answered.

"But, what were those soldiers doing there?" Santiago asked.

"Possibly they were just watching it for amusement. Those people have had ceremonies numerous times over the past several years. They are harmless," she answered.

"What are we going to do today?" Philipe asked, who was bored and wanted to change the subject.

"We are going to look for another place to live," Santiago answered.

"Oh good where?" Philipe inquired, as he squirmed around.

"I have a couple of possibilities, on both St. Philippe and Urseline Streets," he answered, with a smile

"I don't want to be to close to those nuns. If they see me they will try to make me come back and live with them," Philipe said, with disapproval.

"I cannot believe that living with them would be all that bad," Santiago replied.

"Are you trying to make me go back there?" Philipe asked quickly.

"No, of course not," he replied, in a apologetic tone.

"I did not like that school!" Philipe answered back sharply.

Santiago answered him compassionately, "I am not surprised at you saying that, after all everyone at your age does not like school."

"I could not understand what they were saying, the teacher spoke only in Spanish," Philipe responded, in an irritable voice.

"But, now you need to put on your socks and shoes. Then we will go to the horse lot and saddle the horse and ride on St. Philippe," Santiago ordered.

"Why ride, it is only about two blocks?" Philipe asked.

"When the owner of the house sees my fine horse and saddle he will be impressed and think that I have a lot of money. Then he will say to himself, 'This man can pay the rent'," Santiago said, with a big grin.

"This should be interesting," Philipe said, while shaking his head and laughing.

"Why do you make fun of me?" Santiago asked.

"I know some of the people on that street and I think that they will not be so easily misled," Philipe said, pointedly.

Santiago said, somewhat angrily, "So, tell me, just how you could know that."

"Once when I was living at that convent, I ran away. I did not have any food and a day later was very hungry. I knocked on the doors along that street. When the people would come to the door, I would say I was starving and ask for food. They would look at me and say 'You look kind of fat, I don't think you are starving, go away'," he explained.

"In that case we will just have to go and try our luck," Santiago said, with resignation.

They brought the saddle, gathered the horse and saddled it, then both climbed on. They slowly started down the street.

Chapter 32

Very shortly, Santiago and Philipe arrived at the corner of Bourbon and Urseline. Santiago saw a lady working in the flower garden in the front of the house. When she stood up, he saw that she had on a dress with many bustles, but still he could tell she had a nice slender figure. She had heard the horse approaching and turned to see who was coming. When he saw her face, he was not disappointed.

He said to Philipe, "This looks like it has possibilities."

Philipe quipped, "Oh yeah, the woman or the house?"

Santiago looked at him with a scowl as he dismounted and said, "The house of course."

After he got off of his horse he said, "Good morning my name is Santiago and I have been displaced by the fire. I am looking for some thing to rent."

The lady looked up at him and then she looked at Philipe still on the horse.

Santiago saw that she had looked toward the horse so he said, "On the horse is my manservant Philipe and he will be with me."

"That is a nice looking horse and saddle," she said, "Did you buy them here in New Orleans?"

"Yes, I did. I had a nice horse and saddle back home in Catalonia, but I could not bring them on the ship. You have a very nice house. Would you consider renting us a couple of rooms?"

"I am not sure," she answered, hesitantly. "You see, I am a widow."

"I am sorry to hear that," Santiago said. "It appears that you were lucky and did not receive any damage from the fire."

She said while glancing at the house, "Yes, I was blessed."

"I was renting a house from widow Tourneur. Unfortunately, it burned down," Santiago explained.

"I have not been in the habit of renting my rooms, however, because of the fire I understand that there are many who need a place to live," she said.

"We have been in a tent for three days now, and I would very much like to get back into a house," Santiago explained.

"Alright under the circumstances I will rent you the rooms. How does one peso per week in advance sound?" she asked.

"That sounds very reasonable, can I move in right now?" Santiago asked.

"Yes, that will be fine. You can keep your horse in the barn behind the house," she answered.

"Oh by the way my name is Santiago de Barcelona," he said.

"I am Maria Pauley. Are you related to Tomas the Priest?" she inquired.

"Yes, he is my cousin. He arrived here a few years ago," he answered.

"Yes, that will be fine," she answered. "You can keep your horse in the barn behind the house."

"And help yourself to the oats, your horse looks like she can use them," she added.

Santiago replied, "So, you can see her ribs can you? I did not think it was that obvious."

"Only a little," she said smiling.

"Come Philipe, we will put the horse up now," he said.

"That was quick, I thought we would have to go to several houses," Philipe said.

"I think she made a quick decision because she probably needed the money. Also, I saw her looking at my horse and saddle. She appeared to be impressed with them."

"Yes, it is like you said earlier about the appearance," Philipe stated.

"I'll put the saddle over here on this little stand," he said to Philipe. "Be sure to curry her down good, and get those burs out of her tail."

"I think this will be a nice place to stay," Philipe said. "I noticed they have a nice big two seat privy not far from the house. Nice thing to have on those cold mornings."

"It is amazing the way you think of all those little details. Some day you will make a good army sergeant. Now I will get a bucket of water for the trough then we will go inside," Santiago said.

Philipe said, sadly, "I will miss the widow Tourneur."

"I will also," Santiago added. "I will talk to her tonight on my way to meet Diego and tell her where we are now living."

"She will be glad to hear we have found a place," Philipe said.

As the two of them climbed the stairs, they looked back down and noticed what appeared to be two slave girls, each about age fifteen, working around the supper table. When they reached the second floor, they realized that the whole floor had only two rooms.

"Maria was quite generous by letting the two of us live in the whole upper floor of the house, it is very spacious. She and the two slave girls must live on the first floor," Santiago said to Philipe.

Chapter 33

That evening, after Santiago had stopped to see the widow Tourneur, he made his way to Olivier's bistro on the river front. This place had always been a perfect meeting location for he and Diego, two men in the spy business. Also, the friendly manager, Roseta, always made him feel welcome.

As Santiago entered through the open door, he saw her standing in the middle of the room with her hands on her hips. The light in the room was quite dim, lit only by small candles on each table.

"Please come in, my handsome friend. What shall I get for you, a cigar or perhaps a glass of brandy?" she asked in a strong French accent.

She was tall and slender with a very pleasing appearance with curly black hair. He enjoyed looking at her.

"Not right now, I am hungry for some beans and rice, I will have the drink and smoke later. Has Diego been here yet?" Santiago asked.

"I have not seen him today," she said.

He watched her as she bent over the pot to ladle out some of the beans. And he thought to himself, *I wish I could spend more time here.*

Just about that time, who should come walking in the door, but Diego himself.

"Hola, Amigo," he said, in a jovial voice.

This happy-go-lucky personality of his seemed to match his somewhat rotund physique.

"Hola, yourself. You had better get her to fix you a bowl of these beans," Santiago replied.

"Give me what he is having," Diego shouted out loud.

"Si, Señor, coming right up," Roseta answered loudly.

Diego pulled up one of the heavy wooden chairs to the table, swung his right leg over it, and sat down.

Santiago asked, "So, tell me, what is this information that you have to give me tonight?"

"Shhh," Diego answered quietly. "You of course remember when I told you about my contact inside the government here?"

"Yes, I remember," Santiago answered.

"That person delivered to me a very interesting map," Diego said.

All the while holding the bowl of beans just under his chin and shoveling them into his mouth with a spoon.

"Oh, don't tell me, let me guess, it is a map to an old lost gold mine?" Santiago quipped, with a frown on his face.

"No, much more interesting. Here I will show you," Diego answered, while finishing his beans.

As he pushed the empty bowl away, he took out of his waist-band a folded paper and gave it to Santiago. It was slightly tinted as though it had gotten too close to a fire place.

"Hold it down we don't want anybody else to see this," Diego said, as Santiago began to slowly unfold the map.

"Don't worry, there are only two other people in here and they are on the other side of the room," Santiago said, with a grin on his face.

"Yes, I know, but in this town we must be very careful about what we say and do," Diego said in a whisper.

As Santiago looked at the map, Diego was quite for a few minutes.

"Do you see that line printed at the top of the map?" Diego asked, in a whisper.

Santiago answered, "Yes, it says 'Plan of New Orleans in 1770, by Capt. Pittman of the British Army'. Is that the one you are referring to?"

"Oh yes. Notice also, that in the city part there are no houses drawn in," Diego added.

"Yes, I can see that," Santiago answered, with surprise in his voice.

"It would not be possible for anyone to use this map to find the location of the house of any ordinary citizen," Diego explained further.

"Why would Pittman not draw in any of the citizen's houses?" Santiago asked, with curiosity in his voice.

"Your question is a very good one, my friend. To begin with, the only structures that are identified are the guard houses, the powder magazine, the arsenal for boats, prison and outer wall for defense.

"Pittman did not care about the houses. It is, in fact, a military map! One that can be used to plan an assault on this city!"

"It would be very dangerous for you if the army command here knew you had this," Santiago pointed out.

"You are exactly right, both of us would be considered saboteurs and enemy agents trying to launch an attack on this city by the British," Diego replied.

"I must know how you came into possession of this map?" Santiago asked.

"Sorry, my friend I cannot tell you that. If I did then the identity of my inside contact could be compromised," Diego answered.

"But, you and I are spies here only to gather information. We are not planning an invasion by the British," Santiago stated.

"Of course, you and I know that, but the Spanish military authorities, here in New Orleans, would certainly think otherwise,"

Diego replied, "I can guarantee you, we both would be very quickly executed."

"I suppose you are right. Oh by the way, yesterday I saw something unusual at the river's edge that I want to ask you about. There were three ships anchored close together and one was the *Governor Miro*. Does that seem unusual to you?" Santiago asked.

"Yes it does and I will look into that." Diego answered.

Just then he heard Roseta's footsteps coming up behind him, Diego quickly folded the map and put it back into his waistband.

She asked, "Would you gents care for any more brandy?"

Diego answered, "Wish I could stay, but I am late for an appointment now."

He rather quickly got up and rudely brushed passed her and headed for the door.

Just before he walked out, he turned toward Santiago and said, "See you here again tomorrow night."

"How do you like that?" Roseta asked, in an irritated voice.

"Do not take it personally," Santiago said. "That is Diego just being old Diego."

She turned and smiled a big smile at him that seemed to say that she was glad Diego was gone.

She leaned over closely to him with her hand on his shoulder and softly said, "The other customers are all gone now. Why don't we share some brandy together?"

"Can we make that another time?" he asked as he looked into her dark brown eyes. "I am very tired tonight after all of the moving."

"Of course, you know where to find me," Roseta answered.

"Thank you very much for the dinners," Santiago said while putting a small gold Mexican centavo into her hand.

Chapter 34

When he returned to his house that evening the moon was not quiet full, but very bright. This allowed him to avoid the potholes and manure piles in the street, making for a much more enjoyable ride home.

As he entered the house, he quietly proceeded to determine if anyone was still awake. He noticed that there was one of the ladies cleaning the table in the dining area. She was the only one he could see. He assumed the others were in their beds. After reaching the top of the stairs, he walked down the hallway and by Philipe's room. Through the partially opened door, he could see him sound asleep on his bed.

He thought to himself *this would be an opportune time to update the militia information in his notebook.*

While adding the numbers of the soldiers he had seen in the last few days, his eyelids became very heavy. Soon sleep overtook him. He did not realize that his notebook had fallen to the floor.

The next morning he was awakened by the aroma of fresh coffee. While dressing, he remembered that he had not returned the notebook to its hiding place. He looked for it on the floor by the bed, but did not find it. A feeling of panic began to come over him. He looked all around the room for the notebook. Suddenly he spotted it, across the room on top of the table by the window. *That is strange,* he thought, for he did not remember putting it there. As he replaced it to the underside of the top drawer in the table, he thought to himself *I should be more careful.*

But, what if someone had come into the room during the night while he was asleep? What if they had read the notes? Certainly, they would not be able to decipher his code. Perhaps he could ask some not so obvious questions of everyone else in the house.

As he washed his hands and face at the basin he realized that the water pitcher was full now, but that it was not last night. Definitely, someone had been in the room while he was asleep. Quickly he checked all the other papers in his hiding place. They were all there and undisturbed. Maybe I am making too much of nothing. I have other things more important. He put it out of his mind, finished dressing, and went down for breakfast.

"Good morning, everyone," Santiago said, as he descended the stairs.

They were all around the table. Maria Pauley was seated at the head and the two servants were busy setting out the dishes.

"We have a new addition to our household. I think it is someone that you already know," Maria explained.

Just about that time, Juliana entered the dining area from the kitchen outside.

"Hello, Señor Santiago," she said.

She was wearing the dress and new shoes he had bought her.

"My goodness I am so glad to see you. I have not seen you since before the fire. You must tell us what you did during that entire conflagration?" Santiago asked.

"I had gone to see my sister. She and her husband live not far from the hospital. I was there when we saw the fire over in the area of

Toulouse Street. Shortly after that, a strong wind began to blow. We were afraid the blaze would come toward us so we walked down to the edge of the river by the Urseline convent. There were many people along the water escaping the flames. But, it never got close to us. After a short while the wind blew it toward the north," Juliana answered.

"I passed by that area searching for Philipe during the fire and you are right, there were many people by the river escaping the flames. Tonight I will meet with Diego again. Maybe he can add some more information to what we already know," Santiago said.

At Olivier's, Santiago arrived just before Diego. He only just had seated himself at the usual table in the back of the dining area when Diego came in.

"Sorry I am late," Diego said, somewhat breathless. "I was in the process of getting this document from my source."

"Oh really, show me what you got."

He slowly withdrew a large folded piece of paper from his jacket.

"It is a handwritten Declaration by one of the notaries here in the city and dictated by a well known business man, Josef Allemand," Diego answered

"Yes, I can see that," Santiago replied.

"According to this 'the fire reduced to ashes a major portion of the city'. However, I find it curious that the fire is described, but that nothing is said about how it started," Diego stated.

"That sounds like a piece of information we should look into, in a secretive way of course. Would you agree?" Santiago asked.

"Yes, by all means," Diego answered.

"According to this, and my recollection from having been there, it would have started about half-past one in the afternoon and then died out about half-past five later that same afternoon. There was also that very strong wind out of the south," Santiago said.

"I am sorry, but, I must leave you here on your own. I am sure Roseta will be able to take very good care of you," Diego said, as he began to stand up from the table.

"Maybe in two days you will have enough info about the fire so that we can discuss it further?" Santiago asked.

"I will try and get that for you. Yes, I will see you in two days from now," Diego explained, as he walked toward the door.

Chapter 35

S antiago received word through Pedro, two days later, that Diego wanted to meet him on the river bank four blocks west of the Plaza. From there they would ride their horses on Bienville Street toward the River Road.

This time Diego arrived at the meeting place before Santiago.

"I hope you have not been waiting long?" Santiago asked, when he arrived.

"I have been waiting only a few moments, my friend," Diego answered.

"Did you find any information concerning those three ships anchored close together on the river?" Santiago asked.

"Oh yes, those were there the day after the fire because they were being contracted by the Government. That contract stated they were to sail to America, to buy at least four thousand barrels of flour, as well as fruits and vegetables. The original orders were for them to go to New York City, and there, contact the Spanish Envoy Gardoqui," Diego explained.

"New York City, why there?" Santiago asked.

"Good question and that part of the contract turned out to be a problem. The ships were held up one extra day to correct the orders. It seems that the Envoy was actually in Philadelphia, which is the American capital," Diego said.

"That was interesting, but, how were they going to pay for this?" Santiago asked.

"They, being Navarro and Miro, gave the three captains each four thousand pesos, Mexican silver, from the Royal Treasury," Diego answered.

"So, they just went to the Treasury and helped themselves?" he asked.

"Oh no, it was not as simple as that," Diego replied. "The Director of the Treasury, Joseph de Orue, advanced them the money only after each one of them posted a bond to cover that amount."

"How long do you think it will take them to make that trip?" Santiago asked, while looking around to see if anyone was following.

"The trip will take them about forty-five days each way. That is, of course, assuming the weather is good," Diego answered.

"Twelve thousand pesos out of the Royal Treasury is a hefty sum to be floating out on the Atlantic Ocean," Santiago exclaimed.

"You are right, my friend, that is the reason why these contracts are all very hush-hush. There are many privateers out there around the Caribbean Islands who would just love to see these ships coming," Diego said in agreement.

"Have you ever been on one of the pirate ships?" Santiago asked.

"I have not, but some of my acquaintances have," answered Diego.

"This will be good information to pass along, would it not?" Santiago inquired.

"Absolutely!" Diego exclaimed. "You are very perceptive and that statement makes me think you know that the Admiralty finances a lot of those privateers."

"Yes, I know, It is something I found out from a friend in Newgate prison," Santiago replied.

They slowed and looked carefully around the area as they intersected with the River Road.

"To be truthful about this matter, the British have been a problem for the Spanish here in the colony for a long time," Diego said.

"Oh, I did not know it been that bad here," Santiago stated, curiously.

"You see, as recently as 1786 they had made incursions into the territory north and east of New Orleans. Pardon sent out the local militia," Diego replied.

"Was that militia successful?"

"I am not sure about all the details, but yes, they were. Back then my system of contacts were not as sophisticated as they are now," Diego replied.

"That piece of information, plus the fact that Galvez drove the British out of Mobile and Pensacola, would indicate to me that the British are serious about wanting this place back," Santiago suggested.

"Again you are very perceptive, my friend. Also you probably know by now that, if any of the Spanish military suspected us because of who we really work for, then we are in serious trouble," Diego answered.

"I do worry about that," Santiago responded.

"This whole situation concerning information is becoming more complex. Now there is a rumor going around that the fire started in the home of the Treasurer, Vicente Nunez," Diego exclaimed.

"Suggesting that this whole conflagration was caused by some kind of accident?" Santiago asked, loudly.

Diego quickly put his index finger up to his lips. Then they slowed their horses and looked in all directions. Satisfied that no one was in the area they rode on.

"We must discuss this further while we ride back into the city," Diego insisted.

Chapter 36

On their return to the city, they encountered two soldiers on horseback. Diego recognized them as being members of the Spanish fixed regiment, the full time professional soldiers from Catalonia. They were armed with pistols and sabers and stopped near the intersection of Conti and Dauphine Streets. One of them, named Verde, was leaning back in his saddle, his hat was pushed slightly back on his forehead and his right hand on the horse's rump in a very relaxed fashion.

"Hello, Señors de Castellano and de Barcelona," Verde said in a friendly tone.

"Hello, to you two," Diego answered back.

"It is a fine day for a ride, is it not?" Verde asked.

As they drew nearer to the soldiers, they could see that their horses were slightly lathered as though they had been running. Santiago recognized them as the one he had seen before, Teniente Don Pedro Verde and Subteniente Don Luis LaTerreno. Out of fear of raising a question or suspicion, he dared not let on that he knew who they were.

"Say there, are you Santiago, the cousin of Tomas?" Verde asked, in a friendly tone while looking directly at him.

"Yes, I am. Have you seen him recently?" Santiago answered.

"As a matter of fact I did only this morning. We talked for a while and I told him I thought that you were here in the city. So he said 'yes I know, tell Santiago to come and see me when he can'," Verde explained.

"I will do that and thank you for the message," Santiago said, as they slowly walked their horses passed the soldiers.

"Buenas tardes, caballeros," Diego said with a tip of his hat.

After they had gone about a block, they talked about their recent encounter.

"Did you recognize them?" Diego asked Santiago.

"Yes, I did," he answered. "The higher ranking one, Verde, was with the detail that handed out the tents on the night of the fire. I thought that he recognized me then. I knew him from before, back in Barcelona," Santiago answered.

"And the other one?" Diego asked.

"Him I know because someone had pointed him out to me on the street one day," Santiago answered.

"Let me tell you, those two are Pardon's favorites when it comes to special assignments," Diego explained.

"Judging by the sweat on those horses they must have been looking for someone in a hurry, or they were in a rush to catch up to us," Santiago observed.

They rode quietly for a while and Santiago looked out over the city.

"This place looks like a huge army camp with all those tents," Santiago commented.

"Yes, I agree. It will take months, if not years, for these poor people to rebuild their city," Diego stated.

"What was it that you were going to tell me about this complex problem with the fire?" Santiago asked.

"Oh yes, of course," Diego said. "There is a new rumor going around that some of the Frenchmen, who were friends and relatives of those in the rebellion of 1768, still carry a grudge and may have had something to do with the fire getting started. It seems that in years past some of these citizens approached the English north of here. The idea was to have the British annex their part of this colony. Also, there were many English people living in New Orleans at the time O'Reilly arrived. They were in control of the many shops and market places. In so doing, they were taking away about nine-tenths of the market place profit. They also considered Bayou Manchac, in that area north of here, to be a better location for this city than where it is now. They would like very much to have that situation developed."

"So, that is another angle the Brits have to get this place back?" Santiago asked.

"That is correct, my friend or have the city destroyed. Either way they win," Diego explained.

"How could burning the city down possibly benefit those Englishmen?" Santiago asked, with a quizzical look on his face.

"It goes like this, the Spanish are here in this colony only for one reason, and that is to get what they can out of it, such as furs and tobacco, and send that to Spain. They do not care about improving the city and helping the French people, who were here before them. If the city were somehow destroyed then it would no longer be of any value to the Spanish. At that point, they would probably leave. Then the English could build what they want in Bayou Manchac and allow the French to live there too," Diego explained carefully.

"Most of that is clear, but I do not understand how the English and French together would benefit from having a place in Bayou Manchac?" Santiago asked.

"There in that location they could welcome all of the traders coming down the river from the American frontier as well as ships from the gulf. That would add up to a lot of profit for the merchants," Diego answered.

That is certainly an earful," Santiago added. "Were they the only ones with a motive?" Santiago inquired.

"No," Diego answered quickly. "Then there are a group of renegade slaves believed to be here in this colony from St. Dominque."

"And that is it?" he asked in a weary tone.

"For what it is worth, the Spanish have always suspected the Americans. It is obvious, to those with knowledge of the Americans, that they too have had their eye on New Orleans. After all, whoever controls this place also has the rest of the river," Diego said with a smile.

"Why are you grinning?" Santiago asked with a frown.

"I am grinning because, that is all I know," Diego laughed.

"Then who do you think is the most likely suspect?" Santiago asked.

Diego paused for a short moment and then said, "Ask me tomorrow."

Chapter 37

He did not hear from Diego the next day and wondered if something may have happened to him. Diego did mention that he suspected Pardon's men were following him. Then again, maybe all this worrying is just scarring up ghost.

"It is a nice, sunny day, let's go for a ride around the city and look at how things are progressing," Santiago said to Philipe, who had just finished currying his horse.

"I would like that very much sir," Philipe answered, with a smile.

Santiago always liked riding this horse. The saddle had the smell of brand new leather. The horse was sleek and fine and looked like one of those that he used to see in parades in Barcelona.

"Look the piles of burned lumber that were in the streets have been moved," Santiago said to Philipe, as they rode on Dauphine Street toward widow Tourneur's.

"Did everybody come back after the fire?" Philipe asked.

"According to Diego, many went up the river to stay with relatives or friends. When those folks will be back, no one knows for sure," Santiago explained.

"Gosh, that Diego sure does know a lot. Where does he get all that stuff from?" Philipe asked.

"He has well informed friends in high places," Santiago answered.

"Oh, you mean like spies?" Philipe asked, with a big grin on his face.

"Be careful what you say out here in public, some people that hear you make take that seriously," Santiago scolded.

"All right, I won't say that again. How are all those people going to rebuild?" Philipe asked, being full of questions.

"Diego also said that Governor Miro has given all those who had damage, only eight days to turn in a written claim for aid to rebuild," Santiago responded.

Soon they came upon the place where widow Tourneur's house used to be. She was standing next to the tent. The second tent, he and Philipe had used, was gone. The burned timbers, where the house used to be, were now piled to one side of the lot by the street. Grass had started to grow in the center of the lot where soil was scorched.

"Good afternoon widow Tourneur. Has someone been helping you with your cleanup of the debris?" Santiago asked, as he and Philipe dismounted.

"Yes," she answered. "Some of the militiamen from the Pardo Militia Company came by, the other day, and did that for me. They will be back in a few days with a wagon to haul it away."

After Philipe finished tying off the horse, he came running up and put his arm around her.

"Widow Tourneur, how are you?" he asked, with a smile.

"I am fine," she answered, with a bigger smile. "How are the both of you?"

"The place where we live now is nice, it even has a double privy," Philipe blurted out.

"Yes, we have found another place to live, as you know. Are you here all by yourself now?" Santiago asked.

"Yes, the Martines have their own tent now. I see them from time to time. Her headaches finally went away," widow Tourneur explained.

"Have you decided what you will do with your property? Maybe rebuild?" Santiago asked, pointedly.

"I am not quite sure," she answered. "I have not turned in a claim yet."

"Whatever you do I am sure it will be the right thing," Santiago said.

"I should be getting back to the house, Juliana wanted me to go to the mercado with her before supper," Philipe stated.

Santiago and Philipe bid the widow good by and returned to their house.

"Has anyone heard from Diego today?" Santiago asked, after he entered the house.

"Not today," Juliana answered.

"That Diego, he is a sly one," Maria Pauley said.

"Do you know him?" Santiago asked.

"No, but, I have heard many people talk of him and what they say is never good," she answered.

"To tell you the truth, in all our dealings, I have always found him to be trustworthy. I trust him so much, that I have asked him to help me find a good plantation to purchase," Santiago replied.

Even though he said that to Maria, he was just saying it to keep her from discovering the truth about Diego.

The next day, at mid morning, Santiago received a message delivered by Pedro. It said to meet Diego on the river bank near the mercado about an hour after lunch.

Santiago arrived on time at the designated place.

"Hello, my friend" Santiago said to Diego, as he approached him on the river bank. There were many people milling around that area near the market.

"Come let us walk this way," Diego said as he motioned in the direction further down the river.

"Why did you want to meet here?" Santiago asked, as they walked together.

"Olivier's Bistro has probably got officers there. They know it is my favorite place," Diego answered, with a troubled look on his face.

"I notice that you keep looking around in all directions, as though you expect someone to be there," Santiago said.

"I am positive they are following me," Diego said.

"Who is following you?" Santiago asked.

"Pardon's men. Two of them stopped me on the street yesterday and asked me where I was going," Diego answered, with a wild look in his eyes.

"Why would they do that?"

"I think they know who I really am," Diego explained.

"How would they know that? You have been careful haven't you?" Santiago asked.

"Yes, but one of them may have overheard us talking," Diego answered, still appearing to be agitated.

"If that were true then they would know what I am up to also. Would you agree?" Santiago asked.

"Yes, you are right," Diego replied, as he appeared to calm down somewhat.

"Do not look now but, there are two officers on horseback over in that grassy area and they are looking this direction at us," Santiago said quietly.

"Here, take these papers and this map," Diego demanded.

"Okay, but what do you want me to do with them?" Santiago asked.

"Put them in a safe place and if anything happens to me get them to my contact," Diego said, almost begging.

"But, how will I do that? How will I know your contact.?" Santiago enquired.

"We have a previously agreed upon plan, that if I cannot be found she will look for you," Diego said, in a trembling voice and shaking hands.

"What do you mean she?" Santiago asked.

"Do you have a place at your house where I can hide for a few days?" Diego asked, his agitation and trembling now worse.

"Look I can't do that. Taking those papers is one thing, but hiding you, oh no, not a chance. If I were to hide you there and those officers find you, then everybody in the house would go to jail. I know those women, and I tell you, they stick their necks out for no man," Santiago answered in a stern voice, looking Diego straight in the eye.

"Please, you have got to help me!" Diego exclaimed, while holding tightly onto Santiago's arms.

"Look, Diego, I do not know what it is you have done to get yourself into trouble, but I am not going to let you pull me down with you," Santiago exclaimed, as he pushed Diego away forcefully.

"Today one of my contacts at Pardon's office told me that he overheard Pardon and Pound talking about me. He said they know I am a spy. They talked about arresting me," Diego explained, shaking.

Then Diego took off walking fast, back down toward the market area for about fifty paces, at that point he broke into a run and turned left into the city.

Santiago turned toward the officers just in time to see them turn their horses and ride at a slow trot into the city on St. Anne Street. He turned back toward the market area in an effort to warn Diego, but he was already out of sight.

Chapter 38

As Santiago made his way back to the house late that afternoon he noticed some dark clouds forming off in the distance toward the north. He thought how the city did not need more rain at this time.

After entering the house, he walked passed the dining area on his way to the stairs. Sitting at the table was Maria Pauley with some papers in front of her. He smelled the spices from a shrimp boil that had drifted into the house from the kitchen outside. He recognized it as something that Juliana had prepared in the past.

As he reached the top of the stairs he encountered Philipe who had just come out of his room into the hall way.

"Señor, do you know what we are going to have for supper?" he asked in an excited voice.

"Judging by the fine smell I would say it is going to be shrimp," Santiago answered with a smile.

"That would be correct," Maria yelled, from down stairs before Philipe could answer.

"How long before it will be ready?" Philipe asked.

"About an hour," Maria answered.

Santiago immediately went into his room and closed the door as Philipe went down stairs. He thought to himself that *this would be a good time to hide the documents with his notebook.*

Ever since leaving the marketplace he had been preoccupied with the conversation with Diego. The way Diego behaved after the refusal to hide him was totally out of character. He laid on his bed for a while thinking about what might happen next and how he should respond. After an hour, he decided to wash up and go down and join the others for supper.

"This was a wonderful meal, I do not remember when I have had one this good in the past," Santiago commented.

"You can thank Juliana for that," Maria Pauley added.

"You are very welcome," Juliana said, while blushing.

"It is well after sundown and it has been a long and difficult day," he said.

"I will help you clean the dishes," Philipe said quickly to Juliana.

"Why don't you join me in a glass of wine?" Maria asked Santiago.

"I would like that very much," he said smiling.

"Good, this is a very fine Bordeaux that survived the fire," she explained, while she set out the glasses.

Afterwards, she went over to the buffet and blew out the two candles there. This left only the two candles on the table.

"Allow me to pour the wine," he suggested.

"I was hoping that we could find some time, such as this, to get to know each other better," she explained, as she sat down in the chair next to him. The light reflected in her soft green eyes.

"This is perfect. It will help take my mind off of the bad events of the day," Santiago said.

"I think a man should have a place to relax and escape the troubles of the day. Tell me about your day," she said, as she leaned closer.

"That is such a wonderful perfume you are wearing," he said.

To him she looked young and beautiful even though she was a widow.

"I am flattered that you like it," Maria replied while staring into his eyes.

"It is rather complicated," Santiago answered. "It concerns, my friend Diego."

"Oh that fellow. You be careful around him. When trouble happens he always seems to be nearby," she said.

"Today was one of those days," he added.

"You can tell me about it. I am a good listener," she suggested.

"Believe me, I really truly want to tell you," he answered.

They sipped their wine for a short time without saying anything.

"There may be some trouble later tonight or tomorrow," he said.

"Something you have done?" she asked.

"Oh no, not me," he answered.

"Diego then?"

"Yes," Santiago answered.

"Prey tell, what has he done?" Maia asked, in a whisper.

"You see all this time, ever since I met up with him, he was helping me find a plantation. Or so I thought," Santiago explained.

"You mean all this time he was doing something illegal?" Maria asked.

"Yes," he answered.

"I am afraid to ask" Maria said.

"I found out today that he is a spy for the British," Santiago said, in a low whisper.

"And are you?" she asked.

"I came here to buy a plantation, not to get involved with some bunch of international spies," Santiago answered.

"So, you really didn't know what he was up to?" she asked.

"No. What do you think, that I want to get executed?" he asked.

"I know you do not want that," she answered.

"Diego told me today that he knew he was being investigated by Coronel Pardon. He said that one of his contacts in the Infantry overheard Pardon talking to a fella named Pound. They were talking about arresting him."

"So, how does that affect you?" Maria asked.

"Because I have been seen with him at Olivier's," Santiago answered.

"So, what will you do?" Maria asked.

"There is only one thing to do. Explain to them that I am innocent," he answered.

"I know some of the officers in that Regiment and I do not think it will be such an easy a thing for you to do," she replied.

"You really should not concern yourself with my problems," Santiago said.

"It is too late for that, I already care for you," she said.

"It is late and I am sure you are very tired. We both should call it a night," Santiago said.

"You are right, it is time to turn in," she agreed.

As Santiago lay on his bed without sleeping, he could hear the rain begin to fall on the window. All this time he had been wondering what could be going on with Pardon's men. He figured it must be about midnight.

Suddenly there was a loud pounding on the front door.

"OPEN THE DOOR!" someone outside yelled.

He thought that the worst had happened, they had come to arrest him.

"OPEN THE DOOR, this is Capitán de la Dolor of the Infantry Regiment."

Santiago quickly pulled on his pants and shoes and ran downstairs. When he reached the bottom of the stairs, the sight he beheld was more or less, what he expected. The widow had answered the door first. It was wide open and she was standing partially behind it in her housecoat. The look on her face was one of utter terror. She did not say a word.

The capitán was standing in the doorway, behind him was Teniente Pedro Verde, whom Santiago recognized. Behind him was a corporal and two soldiers. These men were not the militia, as he expected to see, but members of the Louisiana Infantry Fixed Regiment, the fulltime professionals. The two officers had pistols in their belts and sabers, while the others had only muskets fixed with bayonets. They were wearing full dress uniforms. These people meant serious business!

The capitán stopped abruptly when he saw the widow. He took off his hat, as did the teniente, and they both nodded.

"Señora Pauley, please forgive this intrusion into your home at such a late hour and allow me to explain," the capitán said.

"Please do," Maria Pauley answered.

"First let me introduce to you Teniente Don Pedro Verde."

"Hello," she said, as he nodded.

"We are here to summon one Señor Santiago de Barcelona to the headquarters for an official inquiry," de la Dolor said, in a formal voice.

"I am Santiago de Barcelona, the one you are looking for," he answered immediately, while stepping forward from the bottom of the stairs.

"Are you armed Señor?" Verde asked.

"No, I am not," Santiago answered.

"You will please come with us," de la Dolor stated bluntly.

"May I please go up stairs and put on the remainder of my clothes?" Santiago asked.

"Certainly," de la Dolor answered. "Verde will accompany you."

As they entered Santiago's room, he felt uneasy about Verde being there. He quickly looked around the room as he gathered his clothes. He could see that the drawer, where the papers were hidden, was well closed and the books, on top of the armoire, were in place. Now he felt more at ease.

They returned downstairs and Santiago was immediately taken out side and put in the back of a wagon with the two soldiers. The corporal sat up front and took the reins. Verde and de la Dolor rode on their horses in front of the wagon.

The rain had stopped and the late night trip was slow going through the wet mud and manure. Upon arriving at a warehouse by the river, one not burned by the fire, he was led inside. There he was placed in a small room, which reeked of the odor of rotting food, and leg irons with chains were attached to his ankles.

"Coronel Pardon will speak with you in the morning. This is the nicest cell we have so make the best of it," said Verde, with a smirk.

After Verde locked the door and walked away Santiago's old memories of Newgate Prison came flooding back.

Chapter 39

It was sometime after sun up that the guard came into Santiago's cell.

"Good morning," he said in a friendly tone, much more friendly than Teniente Verde.

"What is good about it?" Santiago asked, with a snarly voice.

"I was not here when you were brought in last night. What are you charged with?" the guard asked.

"To be truthful I am not sure," Santiago answered.

"In a few minutes you will see the coronel. I am sure he will explain all of it to you," the guard stated.

"Now I really look forward to that meeting," Santiago snapped.

"I think a man who wears the kind of clothes you have on has not spent much time in prison," the guard replied loudly.

"Back about a year or so ago I was a guest of the British Admiralty in London for a few months," Santiago said, laughingly.

"What was the charge?" he asked.

"I was a prisoner of war," Santiago said, nonchalantly.

"Here comes the other guard. Let's take these irons off of you so we can escort you to his office," the guard said.

The coronel's office was but a short distance across the lot from Santiago's cell. Due to the ravages of the recent fire, the inside was somewhat makeshift.

"Sit here," the guard said.

He pointed to an empty flour barrel. The coronel's desk was not much better, a plank laid across the tops of two larger barrels. For light, there were two lanterns, one on each end of the plank. The room reeked with the smell of smoke and old rotting oats.

After a wait of about a quarter of an hour, the coronel entered the room. Initially he said nothing, just looked around and then walked up to the desk. He opened a valise, took out some papers and laid them on the plank. Next, he opened the ink well, took out a very fine quil pen and very carefully put them next to the papers. He was dressed in a formal uniform.

"My name is Coronel Pedro Pardon and I am the Commander of the Louisiana Infantry Regiment. I will be prosecuting this case.

"Santiago de Barcelona, you are being charged with a crime against the Kingdom of Spain and His Royal Majesty King Charles III. To wit: Spying on the Military activities of Spanish Colonial Louisiana while an employee of the British government. How do you plead to these charges?"

"This is absurd!" shouted Santiago. "I say not guilty."

"The investigation is continuing and if more evidence is uncovered you could face more charges. And in that case you will be bound over for trial on those charges as well, which by the way, would be conducted in Havana," Pardon stated further.

"How can you say these things? How can you have any evidence against me? I am not a spy!" He exclaimed loudly.

"Señor de Barcelona these are very serious charges and we do not issue them lightly. If you are found guilty you will most certainly be hanged. Now do you have any questions?" Pardon asked.

"Yes, I want to know just exactly what evidence you have. I am a man of means who came here to buy a plantation, with money from my family. This plantation is to be used to grow indigo and tobacco to be sold to buyers here and in Spain. That has nothing to do with spying," Santiago said.

The whole time Santiago was speaking the coronel was writing on some of the papers.

"Is this the explanation you wish to make?" the coronel asked.

"Yes, and I want to know why you are bringing these charges against me?" Santiago repeated.

"It might interest you to know that we have been keeping you under surveillance since you arrived here by ship. We have a record of everywhere you have gone and with whom you have spoken. The people you have been associated with here will also be rounded up and charged," Pardon responded.

Just as he finished speaking there was a knock on the door. He stood and walked over and opened it only slightly. There was a hushed conversation between he and another officer, who was just outside of the door.

"You are positive? Alright I will be there shortly," he said.

He closed the door and walked back to the makeshift desk.

"We will take a short break while I attend to some other business. Take the prisoner back to his cell and give him something to eat," Pardon commanded.

Back in his cell they gave him a bowl of rice and beans and some wine, but not enough to make him drunk. He felt more relaxed after he ate, but still concerned about their evidence.

Back in Pardon's office, the coronel brought in more papers with him when he returned.

"Are you acquainted with a man by the name of Diego Castellano?" Pardon asked.

Chapter 40

Santiago explained, "Yes, I am acquainted with Señor Castellano."

"Is it true that the two of you have met on a regular basis, every few days, since you arrived?" Pardon asked.

"Yes, that is also true," Santiago answered.

"Do you also know a free woman named Roseta, the manager of Olivier's?" Pardon asked, while lighting up a rather large Cuban cigar.

"Yes, she has always been kind to me," he answered, while thinking *I wish I had a cigar like that one.*

"We know that you are acquainted with a free pardo named Pedro. Is it not true that he occasionally carried messages between you and Diego?" Pardon asked, while pacing back and forth across the room.

"Yes, in much the same way that he served drinks at your Christmas Party," Santiago retorted.

"RUDE AND INDIGNANT ANSWERS WILL NOT HELP YOUR CASE AT ALL SEÑOR!" Pardon yelled at Santiago, while the guards snickered.

Pardon quickly turned his stare toward the guards. They rapidly clicked their heels together and stood at attention.

"Yes, sir," Santiago responded.

"I have right here, on this paper, all the names of the people in the ring of spies that you and Diego have set up," Pardon said, while shaking the paper in front of Santiago's face. "This is enough information to send you to that Morro Castle prison in Havana, right now."

"I tell you that I know nothing about any spies," he answered. "It is like I said before. I am here to buy a plantation, nothing more."

There was another knock on the door, again interrupting Pardon's interrogation of Santiago. After speaking to another officer for a few minutes outside the door, he came back in.

"Guards bring the prisoner," Pardon said. "We are going to the small building next door."

Both of the guards stood one on each side of Santiago, holding their muskets with bayonets fixed in the shoulder position. As they approached the building, he noticed three buzzards circling around the grassy area between the buildings. Inside it was dark and the guards had to light some candles.

"All right pull back the cover," Pardon ordered one of the guards.

"Oh no!" Santiago exclaimed in a low tone as he saw that underneath the sheet was the body of Diego. Very real and very dead. There was a rather large knife cut across his abdomen.

"Do you recognize this man?" Pardon asked.

"Yes, Santiago answered."

"Tell me his name, Pardon commanded."

"Diego Castellano," Santiago replied.

"Maybe that is his name. Then again maybe not," Pardon suggested. "But, what ever it is we will eventually find out."

"When did he die?" Santiago asked.

"About two days ago," Pardon answered.

Pardon walks over and stands next to Santiago while he is still looking at the body.

"As you have seen, in New Orleans life is cheap," Pardon said with a smirk.

"DID YOU KILL HIM?" Santiago yelled at Pardon as the two guards grabbed Santiago and pulled him back.

"No Señor, you did," Pardon said, in an accusing tone.

"Are you crazy, he was, my friend. He was helping me find a plantation," Santiago said.

"Our investigation shows that he had a great deal of money on him about two days ago. When we found him, his pockets were empty. We searched his room and found only six reales. Then, we searched your room. Guess what? We found three hundred seventy-five Pesos, Mexican silver," Pardon explained.

"I did not steal that money!" Santiago exclaimed forcefully.

"You were seen with him later that day when he had the money," Pardon stated.

"That money was given to me by my family before I left Cadiz, Spain," Santiago said.

"I advise you Señor, you had better start telling the truth. Then maybe I can help you in this situation. Otherwise there is a very good possibility you will wind up like your friend here," Pardon said, with a smirk. "Take him back to his cell."

As they walked him back across the grass, he looked up in the sky to see that now there were five buzzards.

In the little cell, they put the leg irons back on him. Before the guards left, one of them turned to him.

"It does not look good for you Señor. If they find you guilty of this murder then they might just hang you right here."

"And how is it that you know such things?" Santiago asked.

"It is the buzzards, sir, they do not lie," the guard answered, while pointing a finger toward the sky.

Santiago thought to himself, *Maybe I will never be able to convince them I did not kill Diego. Maybe they have more faith in these signs than real evidence. Also maybe I will not be able to convince them that I am not a spy. I feel doomed.*

Chapter 41

He thought that the next time he would talk to Pardon he would counter their claims of his guilt by using various suggestions. *But, what suggestions would that be? Maybe if I could talk to my cousin Tomas. He has always been very wise. But, how would I get word to him?*

"Guard, oh guard," he called at the door.

"Yes?."

"Do you know the priest named Tomas de Rodrigo?"

"I do."

"Is there some way that I can get a message to him?"

"Of course, I can take it to him. I can do that when my shift ends shortly."

"Just tell him that I am in here and need to see him."

"Here comes my relief now. I will take the message."

Santiago walked back over to the corner where he had been sitting. Thinking how embarrassed he will be when Tomas sees him. *It cannot be helped, I need to have someone to help me. I need to talk to someone.*

That evening Tomas came to see Santiago in his cell.

"It grieves me greatly to see you in here," Tomas said.

"Hello, cousin," Santiago said.

"The guard did not give me any information. Tell me, my son, why are you here?" Tomas asked.

"I have been accused of spying, robbery and murder," Santiago answered.

"Are you guilty of these crimes?" Tomas asked, while putting his hands on his shoulders.

"No, not all," Santiago answered, after a short pause.

"You can lie to yourself, but you cannot lie to God," Tomas said.

"I did not kill and rob Diego," he said, quietly just above a whisper.

"And what else?" Tomas asked.

"I worked for a short period of time, after I arrived here, delivering messages for Diego to his British friends," Santiago explained.

"And how did you come to know this Diego?" Tomas asked.

"I looked him up because I wanted him to help me find a place to live," Santiago said.

"So, what else?" Tomas inquired.

"The second time we met, supposedly to talk about a house, he asked me if I wanted to make some extra money," explained Santiago. "I said sure why not."

"Go on," Tomas said.

"He said that if I took some letters to a friend of his in Bayou Manchac, he would pay me twenty pesos. Also that if I delivered them on time we could do this on a regular basis," Santiago answered.

"So, that is all there was to it?" Tomas asked.

"Yes. I honestly do not know who killed him," Santiago answered.

"Did the officers have any proof that you killed him?" Asked Tomas.

"They found money in my room and they say that it belonged to him. But, it was given to me by him for delivering the letters," Santiago explained.

Tomas consoled him by saying, "I will do what can be done for you. Before I go we shall pray."

During this whole conversation, Verde had been on the other side of the wall. He had found an old knot hole very close to where Santiago was sitting. No one had seen him there as he listened to everything that was said. At the end of their talk, Verde got up and went into Pardon's office to report what he had heard.

"What have you got for me?" Pardon asked.

"It was as you suspected. He confessed to the Priest," Verde answered. "But, only for the spying. He denied the killing and robbery."

"That Priest did not happen to see you did he?" Pardon asked in a serious tone.

"No, sir, I was very careful," Verde answered.

"Very interesting," stated Pardon.

"Another interesting piece of information came out during their talk. This Diego, he had friends in Bayou Manchac, just north of here," added Verde.

"Yes, well good. Once Pound told me that he suspected that," Pardon said, and smiled as he lit another cigar.

"Maybe we will get to send him to Havana after all," Verde stated, with a wide grin on his face.

"Yes, my friend, but I think we need a little more information," Pardon said.

There was a knock on the door. It was Capitán de la Dolor with some new information.

"Two of the Pardos on patrol caught two libres trying to break into the home of Don La Chiapella," de la Dolor explained. "On interrogation they claimed they were going to split the loot, what ever they could get, with Pedro."

"I hope you have more than that," demanded Pardon.

"Oh, yes. They also claim to have information about the murder of Diego," de la Dolor added.

"This is a most interesting turn of events!" Pardon exclaimed smiling. "What do you know about these two?"

"I would have to say that neither one of them appear to be the sharpest knife in the drawer, so to speak," de la Dolor answered.

"That is also very interesting," exclaimed Pardon. "Go and lean on them some more. See if you can extract any details about the Diego murder."

"Yes, sir, Coronel," answered de la Dolor, as he left the room.

"Verde," said Pardon. "Bring me Santiago, I wish to discuss some new charges against him."

When Santiago arrived, he was greeted by Pardon.

"Have a seat, we have more information about the Diego murder. It seems you were overheard saying that you were going to kill him."

"That is not possible! I saw him the day you arrested me."

"Did you two part on good terms?"

"Yes, well no," he stammered. "You see he was very upset about something, but he could not tell me. Then he ran away. I did not see him alive again after that. A little while later I went back to the house."

"Is that when you hid the money in your room?" Pardon asked.

"NO! I told you that money came from my family," Santiago answered sharply.

"That is not a very convincing story Señor," replied Pardon. "I must tell you that we have a witness that overheard your comment about killing Diego. He is willing to swear to it in front of a Notary."

"IT IS SIMPLY NOT TRUE I TELL YOU!" Santiago yelled. "I do not understand why these people are doing this."

"Since you do not want to change your story we will send you back to your cell. Maybe by tomorrow you will come to your senses," Pardon stated.

"Okay, let's go back to your cell," Verde said, grinning as led him away by the arm.

Santiago felt very depressed now. His attempts to counter Pardon's claims had failed. He thought *my only hope now is that somehow the true killer of Diego will be found. But who, when, why and how?*

As they were leaving, Santiago noticed de la Dolor going into Pardon's office

Chapter 42

Pardon asked. "What information do you have for me, Capitán?"

de la Dolor said, "One of the fellows we picked up is willing to make a deal with us. He says if we promise to give him a lighter sentence he will tell us all the details, including how Pedro killed that hombre Diego."

"You cannot be serious!" Pardon replied loudly.

"Yes, sir, I am," de la Dolor answered.

"This testimony has the power to change many things," Pardon stated, while puffing on a cigar.

"What is our next step, Coronel?" de la Dolor asked.

"Here is what I want you to do. First: Go and get one of the escribanos (scribe) from Governor Miro's office. Take him into the interrogation room so he can write down everything that fellow has to say. This must be done in front of two witnesses. Second: Interrogate the other fellow. If he confesses, then have that taken down in writing also. Third: If they both implicate Pedro, and I think they will, then immediately arrest Pedro on suspicion of murder and robbery, also search Pedro's house for the money. Fourth: Then we will change the charges against Santiago," Pardon explained.

"That is a lot to do and it is getting to be late afternoon. Should we work through the night?" de la Dolor asked.

"Absolutely," Pardon answered sharply. "We must get all these people locked up as soon as possible."

Just before sunrise de la Dolor returned to Pardon's office with the signed confessions.

"Here are the documents just as you ask for," de la Dolor said.

"Very good, Capitán," the coronel said.

"Now, I will take two men with me and go arrest this Pedro. After that I will have some breakfast, then I will take the men to search Pedro's house, and anywhere else he might have hidden the money," de la Dolor explained, in a tired voice.

"After you finish with Pedro, report back to me. Then you may take two days off," Pardon said, with a smile.

"Yes, sir!" de la Dolor replied, in a snappy voice and a smile.

About two hours later de la Dolor returned to Pardon's office.

"We have Pedro in one of the cells in irons. I have already questioned him about the murder and the money. He denied the murder. He says he has no money and that he is broke. Then I showed him the money bag we found in his cart outside of his house. The bag had the initials D.C. on the outside and on the inside were four hundred twelve silver pesos. He did not say anything else after that," de la Dolor explained.

"The evidence is clear," began Pardon. "We will charge him with murder, the motive being robbery."

"Here is the bag, sir, and I will go now."

"You have done a very good job. You deserve a good rest," Pardon said, with a big smile.

"On the way out please tell Teniente Verde to come to my office."

"Yes, sir," said Verde, as he entered the office. "You sent for me?"

"How are you this morning?" he asked.

"Ah, fine sir," Verde stammered. "But, it is afternoon."

"Oh my, last night was a long one," Pardon replied. "I want you to go and get Santiago and bring him here. You might as well know we are going to drop the charges of murder and robbery against him."

"That is good news," Verde replied. "I am sure Santiago will be glad to hear that."

"Of course the charge of spying will still be pending against him," Pardon added.

"I will get him and return shortly," Verde stated, "While you were busy with Capitán de la Dolor, a Mr. Pound came by to see you," the guard at the door explained. "He asked if you were available. I told him that you were occupied. He said he would return tomorrow."

"Did he say what he wanted?" Pardon asked.

"No, sir," the guard answered.

"Okay, thank you," Pardon said, with a puzzled look on his face.

"Come in," Pardon answered, responding to a knock on the door.

"I have Santiago," Verde said.

"Good bring him in," the coronel said.

"If you are going to ask me if I have changed my mind, don't bother," Santiago said abruptly, while standing in front of the coronel's desk.

"Frankly, Santiago, I have good news for you. The charges against you of the murder and robbery of Diego Castellano have been dismissed. Evidence, discovered over the last two days by Capitán de la Dolor, has cleared you of that charge," Pardon explained.

"Is someone else to be charged?" Santiago asked , in an excited tone.

"Not at this time," Pardon answered. "The investigation has not been concluded yet. When it is then I will be happy to answer your question."

"I see," replied Santiago.

"Do you have any further questions?" asked Pardon.

"No," answered Santiago.

"You will be returned to your cell now," Pardon ordered.

Chapter 43

After lunch, Verde returned to Pardon's office for his next assignment. He found the coronel sitting in his chair with his feet up on the desk top, smiling while smoking a cigar and belching from the large lunch he just consumed. When Verde observed the coronel's good mood, he took the opportunity to ask him a question.

"Sir, may I ask you about the case against Santiago that we just concluded?"

"Why of course," Pardon answered, with a smile.

"How did you know Santiago was innocent of the murder and robbery charge?"

"I will tell you how that happened. The reason that I am going to tell you is because it will show how I worked this case. That will be of benefit to you in the future. It will make you a much better investigator as well as an officer," Pardon began, as he blew cigar smoke into the air and stroked his mustache with his index finger.

"Oh yes, sir, that will be great," Verde said, with a smile.

"First of all we have been keeping a dossier on Santiago ever since he arrived from Cadiz, Spain. We also had an extensive one on Diego."

"How did you know he was coming?"

"We had been watching Diego for some time and noticed he had paid Pedro money. Exactly for what, we did not know. We started following Pedro. Every day when a ship would come in at the river, he would meet it with his cart as though he was looking for someone. When one of the crew would put out the plank to unload, Pedro would talk to him. He appeared to be asking him some questions. Several days, more than a week I think, went by and Pedro did not find that person. Finally when the ship *Adriana* arrived he found his man."

"So, Pedro knew Diego for some time. Even had financial dealings with him did he not?" Verde asked.

"Yes, you are very observant," Pardon answered.

"All of my capitánes are aware of the dossiers that we keep on certain individuals. When Capitán Don Pedro Fontaine was visiting with his friend Don Andres Burns, Santiago was there and purchased one of Burns's horses. Fontaine just happened to be sitting on the porch close enough to hear what they were saying. As a matter of fact he was also close enough to see Santiago's fancy leather money pouch. The one with the initials S B on it and from which Santiago took out the silver coins to pay Burns. After the transaction, Burns told Fontaine 'that fellow has money'. The next day Fontaine recorded all this in Santiago's dossier."

"How do you find time to read all those dossiers?" Verde asked.

"Usually not that difficult. You see, I only read the ones which have new entries that day."

"So, he bought the horse with money that he brought with him from Spain, right?" Verde asked.

"That is very true. We have no record of him having any occupation, but he seemed to always have money and nice clothes," Pardon stated.

"Was there more?" Verde questioned.

"Oh, yes. One afternoon after Santiago had purchased the horse, he and Diego went riding on the river road by the old Jesuit plantation. An officer followed them at a distance, not close enough to hear, but close enough to see. At one point, they stopped and dismounted. Diego gave him an old leather pouch, which appeared to be heavy. My man was hiding in the brush behind a tree and he accidentally stepped on a twig. This scared the horses, which in turn alerted our two subjects. They mounted up with their pistols drawn and rode off.

"It has been inferred that the old leather bag contained silver pesos. The next day one of Fontaine's men found an empty old leather bag in a trash pile outside of Santiago's rooming house on Dauphine Street. This suggested Santiago must have transferred the coins to the new pouch that day."

"How did you find the new pouch with the money after he was arrested?" Verde inquired.

"When he was arrested the pouch was not on him. We knew it had to be somewhere in Maria Pauley's house. Initially, when we searched the room, we could not find anything. Then we noticed that there were some books on top of the armoire. That seemed to be an odd place to put books. On closer inspection, up there, we found the pouch. That hiding place would make sense though, he is over six feet tall and that would be easy for him to reach. The other people living in that house were shorter and would not be able to see that high."

"So, your conclusion at that point was that he was a spy?"

"Yes, because of his close relationship with Diego, we always suspected he was a spy. But, then Diego shows up dead. Not only is he dead, he has no money. Diego's dossier suggested he was never broke. So that part did not add up. As I said earlier, Santiago also had money. At that point I was not convinced Santiago was the murderer," Pardon stated.

"Then Santiago sent for Tomas. I overheard their conversation and reported it back to you," added Verde.

"Yes, that conversation did a great deal to convince me that he was innocent of murder. He told the priest that he was a spy, but he did not kill and rob Diego. Santiago is a very religious man and when he said that to the priest, he was convinced that he was talking to God. He could not lie at a time like that."

"But, you did not drop the charges then. Why not?" asked Verde.

"I had to tie up four loose ends. It was necessary to have signed confessions from the two friends of Pedro. I also needed to have the money pouch that belonged to Diego and account for the money. Finally, with all of the above evidence, we confronted Pedro. After that I gave de la Dolor two well deserved days off."

"I hope some day that I will be as good an investigator as you," stated Verde.

"I am sure you will be. Now it is time to call it a day. Tomorrow morning we will discuss with Santiago the remaining charges against him. Then we can plan his trip to Havana," Pardon said.

Chapter 44

All that night there were chains around Santiago's ankles. It was impossible to get any sleep with them cutting into his legs. The mosquitoes made his problems even worse. They were abundant and terrible and there were no nets to keep them away.

The next morning the guards fed him early, a piece of bread, a boiled potato and water. After that, they escorted him to Pardon's office. He was made to sit on the same old barrel directly in front of the coronel's makeshift desk. The two guards stood by the door, one on each side with muskets and fixed bayonets. There were two long sheets of paper on the desk in front of Pardon. He picked up one of them and began to read it.

"We are here this morning to lay out before you the two options you have concerning the charge of being a British spy against the Kingdom of Spain and His Majesty King Charles III in the Spanish Colony of Louisiana.

"First, if you confess to this crime and reveal your associates, and all activities since you arrived in New Orleans, then there is a very good possibility that you will be imprisoned here in this city for the term of your sentence.

"Second, if you do not confess, but instead claim innocence to the charge, then we will have to send you to the higher authorities in Havana, Cuba. You will be tried in their court. If found guilty, there is a good chance you will be hanged.

"Santiago de Barcelona do you understand the charge against you?" Pardon asked.

"Yes, I understand," Santiago answered quietly.

"How do you plead, guilty or innocent?" Pardon asked loudly.

Suddenly, before Santiago could answer, there was a very loud pounding on the door. Everyone turned their heads in that direction. One of the guards opened the door. The man on the other side of the door spoke something to him, but Santiago could not hear it. The guard motioned for the coronel. Pardon walked over and spoke to the man in the doorway. They talked for several minutes, Pardon occasionally pointing in Santiago's direction. Finally, Pardon stepped outside and shut the door behind him.

About ten minutes went by and Pardon came back inside. Santiago could see that the man was gone. The coronel sat at his desk opened a folder with some papers in it and then wrote something on them.

"We will have to finish this later today. Guard, return the prisoner to his cell," Pardon ordered abruptly.

It was after the noon meal when Santiago was brought back to the coronel's office.

"I have received word from the governor through Mr. Pound, that there has been a major change in plans with the prosecution of your case. To be clear on the subject, your prosecution is going to be suspended for the time being," Pardon stated.

"Will I have to remain in chains in the warehouse?" Santiago asked, in an anxious tone.

"That is what I need to explain to you."

"I feel better about this already," Santiago stated, with a smile.

"Do not get too excited just yet. You have not been given any freedom. However, that could change depending on how you answer the following questions." Pardon stated.

"Oh, I see," answered Santiago.

"Let me begin by saying this, the governor and his closest staff have come to the conclusion that the colony, at present, does not have an adequate number of personnel in the area of clandestine operations," Pardon explained.

"I suppose you are referring to people in my line of work?" Santiago asked.

"Exactly. They instructed me to ask if you would be interested in working for us in that capacity. Are you interested in hearing the details?" Pardon asked.

"Yes, of course, if I will receive something in return."

"The plan is this: Your case will be suspended just as I already have said. If you agree then you will be placed on a form of close supervision. During that time, you will be given the assignment of acting in the role of a double agent. You will continue to work for the British just as before. Making sure that you quickly establish a new contact with them. This will include receiving the usual salary from them. During this time, you will also be working for us.

"To prevent them from finding out what we are doing a cover story will be circulated around the city that you have been released for lack of evidence. In addition to that, another story will be circulated that you have signed a contract to buy a plantation not far from here on the river," Pardon explained.

"Go on, this is beginning to sound very interesting," Santiago stated.

"For the time being you will continue to stay at the widow Pauley's," Pardon explained.

"Will I receive any salary from the colony?" Santiago asked.

"Yes, exactly how much is yet to be decided," Pardon answered.

"Will I be allowed to have my money back? You know the pouch you took from my room," Santiago inquired.

"Yes, that would be reasonable, replied Pardon."

"And my horse, saddle, and my gun?" asked Santiago.

"Yes," Pardon agreed.

"I am already to go," Santiago said.

"Not so fast. Technically you have not yet agreed," Pardon shot back quickly.

"Yes, I agree," replied Santiago humbly.

"Later you will declare that formally in front of Pound and myself. For security purposes there will be no written documents associated with your activities," Pardon explained.

"I understand," answered Santiago.

"At the present time you will contact either de la Dolor or myself. That however, may change in the future," explained Pardon.

"May I be allowed to ask a question at this point?" asked Santiago.

"Yes," answered Pardon.

"I was under the impression that the colony had enough people in this business. Was that wrong?" Santiago asked.

"Without going into detail I can say that in the last few weeks we have noticed what appears to be an increase in foreign agents in the city. We are not sure if they are English or American. That is all I can tell you about that," answered Pardon.

"Thank you," said Santiago.

"I am going to cover one more important point. One that all three of us, the governor, Pound and myself, agree on. We will be keeping a very close eye on you all the time. One little mistake, one failure to follow orders, even giving the appearance of such, and we will drag you back in here. We will lock you in irons again and put you back in that warehouse and continue with your prosecution!" Pardon stated forcefully.

"Do not worry, sir, I understand," Santiago answered.

"Now I must say this, you have something going for you. You are Spanish like us, you know our customs and speak our language. You are also familiar with the opposition. This is what made you look appealing to Pound, so take my advice and make the best of that," Pardon explained.

"I will do that. What happens now?" Santiago asked.

"Your first assignment will be to connect with your new British contact. After that, one of us will contact you to get a report. Then we will take it from there. I suspect most of your activities will be on a day to day basis. So stay on your toes," Pardon ordered.

"Is that it then?" Santiago asked.

"No, in about an hour Pound, you and I will meet here and formalize that verbal agreement," answered Pardon.

"I am ready " declared Santiago.

"After that you will verbally give me all the names of your British contacts. How many times you met with each contact and the details of those discussions. If you have taken down any notes about Spanish activities, you will be required to turn those over to me within one days time. Do not attempt to make copies of those notes. That would be a serious breach of our agreement.

"Then, after all of that is concluded, we will return your possessions that were confiscated and you will leave the building on foot and walk back to your rooming house. And remember your success in this operation will be entirely up to you," Pardon reaffirmed.

"Yes, sir," Santiago answered.

Chapter 45

At the appointed time Santiago, Pardon, and Pound arrived at Pardon's office. There was no one else present. Pardon recited the agreement as he had written it on a piece of paper. Each responded by saying, "I agree," at that point, he held up the paper and very carefully raised the candle to one of the corners of the paper. He allowed it to fall into a large ashtray on his desk. It was quickly consumed. They each took a seat for the remainder of the meeting.

Pardon took out a sheet of paper and inked his quill.

"Now tell me your activities beginning with the time prior to your departure from Cadiz, Spain," he ordered.

As Santiago gave out the precise details, Pardon quickly wrote them down. After about two hours, Pound excused himself from the meeting saying, "I must leave now for a meeting with Governor Miro, I will read your report later."

Pardon and Santiago continued for several more hours. When they had finished the sun had already set. It appeared to Santiago that the coronel had written almost fifty pages.

"It is dark outside, is there anything else you need from me?" Santiago asked.

"No, not that I can think of. Now is a good time for you to leave," Pardon suggested.

"May I have my belongings now?"

"Yes, of course. Here is your pistol, unloaded of course, and your money pouch."

Santiago quickly counted the coins.

"Well?" Pardon asked, gesturing with his hands in the air.

"It is all there. I will return tomorrow morning with the notes."

As he walked from the warehouse to Maria Pauley's rooming house, he felt greatly relieved. However, he thought how, for the second time in his life, he had managed to dodge that fatal bullet. This is not something he wanted to repeat ever again.

As he walked up the street toward the house, he was able to see where he was going by the light from the lanterns on the front of houses along that street. As he arrived at the front of the rooming house, the door was closed. It was after supper time and it seemed quite. He knocked very softly.

"Señor Santiago you are back," Philipe stated, as he opened the door.

"Yes, I am free now. How are you?" Santiago asked.

"We are all fine, but we have been worrying about you," Philipe answered.

"I know you have been. I was worried myself," Santiago replied.

"You have to tell me all about what happened," Philipe demanded excitedly.

"I will, but I want to say hello to everybody?"

"They are all out back in the barn, one of Maria's mares is having a colt. I will go and tell them you are here, they all will be excited," Philipe said, with wide eyes.

"While you go to the barn I will go upstairs to my room. By the way, it is important that you always refer to Maria as widow Pauley," Santiago instructed.

"Yes, sir, I will," he answered.

He slowly climbed the stairs to his room. Fatigue had begun to set in. Events of the last few days were beginning to release their emotional grip on him. After reaching the top, he had to think twice before remembering which room was his. Even though one hour had passed since he left the coronel's office, it seemed like a day.

Standing beside his bed he unconsciously dropped his gun and money pouch. Then he heard the door close behind him. He turned and was surprised the see Maria walking toward him and her eyes were red.

"I am so glad you are back home safe with us," she said, wrapping her arms around him and laying her head on his chest. He instinctively put his arms around her also.

"It feels wonderful to be here with you too. At one point I thought I was going to be sent to prison in Havana," Santiago admitted.

"I had gotten used to you being around. I would be so sad if you had not come back," she explained in a quiet voice.

Suddenly he tried to turn, but his right leg was too close the side of the bed. The next thing he knew they both had fallen onto the bed, her on top of him. She looked into his eyes and kissed him like she had never kissed any man before. He put his arms around her and drew her close to him.

"Señor, Señor," Philipe said in a loud voice as he knocked on the door. "The mare, she has had a filly."

"I guess we will have to finish this at another time," Santiago said.

"Are the mare and the colt okay?" Maria Pauley asked Philipe.

"Yes, they are both standing up," Philipe answered.

"In that case we can all go to supper now and check on them later," she said.

They both smiled as they got up and headed down stairs. Maria going ahead of Philipe and Santiago.

"Why were the two of you in your bed?" Philipe asked in a whisper.

"I will explain that later," Santiago said sternly.

At the table while eating, Santiago explained his version of what happened. He led them to believe that the only reason for him to be detained was because they suspected him in Diego's death. He gave them none of the other details.

The next morning after an early breakfast, he had Philipe saddle his horse and then he left for Pardon's office. With him were the notes he had promised. As he approached the warehouse, he felt it would be best to leave his horse at one of the stables adjacent to the mercado two blocks away. He did not know if he was being watched, but did not want to take any chances. As he left the stable, he walked into the crowded area of people buying and selling. Moving slowly as though looking for something to buy he eventually made his way to the other side. Walking slowly down the block he came to the warehouse and paused, looking this way and that. Not seeing anyone near, he entered.

"Good morning Santiago," Pardon said with a slight smile. "Do you have something for me?"

"As you ordered, here are the notes," Santiago said, as he handed over the small notebook.

"Very good, I will review these later," Pardon said. "Now before I go over your assignment do you have any questions?"

"Yes, I do. I am quite worried what would happen to me if the British find out that I am a double agent. I think they would want to murder me just for revenge. Maybe even torture me to make me give information on you and your operation," Santiago said, in a worried tone.

"I can tell you that with any military activity involving contact with the enemy there will always be the chance of physical danger," Pardon explained.

"Yes, of course. I am worried that they may find out about the notebook. After all, when I meet with them I will not have it," Santiago said.

"Precisely," Pardon stated. He reached into his valise and took out a small notebook, almost identical to the one Santiago turned in. He handed over to him.

"What am I supposed to do with this?" Santiago asked

"Open it and read some of the pages," Pardon suggested

There were notes, similar to Santiago's, but different. The hand writing was oddly similar to his own.

"This is absolutely crafty!" Santiago exclaimed.

"That is the notebook you will use from now on. From time to time, we will update the pages. The information in there is partly true and partly false. It is designed to be true enough to get them interested, but false enough to mislead them. Overall, in the end it will be of no value to anyone. They will not realize that for some time to come," Pardon explained.

"I see, you fellas are clever," Santiago stated.

"Yes, we have been at this business for quite some time. This will not be the first time we have fed misleading information to the British. As a matter of fact, it, came in very handy in General Galvez's campaign in the taking of Mobile and Pensacola," Pardon said boastfully.

"I must say I am very impressed," replied Santiago.

"Now as far as your personal safety is concerned. We are going to issue you another pistol, one that is very modern. It uses the firing cap to ignite the powder. Much faster at reloading and safer. It will also fit in your hand much better than that old dueling piece you now carry. Use that one for a backup. Always keep your knife handy.

"You may have noticed that Portuguese ship anchored in the river on the day you arrived. It is manned by British agents posing as Portuguese sailors. They are nothing more than a bunch of old pirates, cut throats, every last one of them," Pardon explained.

"You sound like you know them very well," Santiago observed.

"I do. I have dealt with their kind before," Pardon replied.

"I won't ask when or where," Santiago said.

"I recommend that you modify you speech to try and match theirs as much as possible," Pardon said.

"I am sure I can do that," Santiago agreed.

"Someone will be watching you day and night. You will probably not recognize him. If a situation develops, such as you being attacked, then that man will help you," Pardon assured him.

"That is good, makes me feel better," Santiago stated.

"In addition, we will give you sixty pesos per month, starting now," Pardon explained.

"Now that is something I really like!" Santiago exclaimed.

"You are also to occasionally visit Olivier's. Go there during the busy time of day. Make sure Roseta, as well as other people, see you," Pardon explained, in somewhat of a monotone.

"I am beginning to like this job more and more," Santiago stated, with a smile.

"You will have to be flexible, plans can change at any moment."

"That should be easy enough," stated Santiago.

"That is about it for now. Go back to your boarding house. Someone will contact you in a day or so with precise instructions," ordered Pardon.

Chapter 46

He carefully walked to the stable where he left his horse, checking several times to see if anybody was watching him. After a slow ride back to the boarding house, he put his horse in the barn, continuing to look over his shoulder from time to time. He began to think how he feels more insecure now than when he left the coronel's office two days earlier. Now would be a good time to check out that new pistol.

As he entered the barn, someone spoke to him from a distance.

"Señor, have you been for a ride?" Philipe asked as he came walking up behind him.

"Only a short one," replied Santiago.

"Oh wow, you have a new pistol," Philipe observed.

"Yes, it is a nice one. It used to belong to Diego," Santiago answered.

"How did you get it?" Philipe asked.

"The officers gave it to me for protection," Santiago answered.

"Will you show me how to use it sometime?" Philipe requested.

"Yes, of course.   What has been going on around here this morning?" Santiago asked.

"A man came by, he was not a blacksmith, but the one who works on the horses hooves," Philipe stated.

"Oh, you mean the Ferrier," replied Santiago.

"Yea, that is what he is called," Philipe answered.

"What did he want?" asked Santiago.

"He said he had heard that we had a new filly and that he would be happy to check the mare for us," Philipe explained.

"The widow told him to come back this afternoon when you were here" Philipe answered, while he drew "X" marks in the dirt with his shoes.

"If I saw him how would I know him?" Santiago asked.

"He had a wagon full of tools," Philipe answered.

"Just like the one this fellow has coming here now?" Santiago asked, pointing to the wagon in the street.

"Yea, that's him," replied Philipe.

"While I work with him on the mare you go help Juliana. I'm sure she can use some help getting supper ready," Santiago ordered.

"Aw shucks, I wanted to watch you guys," Philipe said, as headed for the kitchen.

"My name is Carlos," the man said as he reached out his hand to Santiago.

"Nice to meet you, my name is…."

"Santiago. Yes, I know," Carlos interjected. "I heard around town that you now have a nice new filly."

"Yes, come over here I will show you," Santiago said, as he lead Carlos into the barn.

Carlos lifted up the right forefoot of the mare as if he were looking for something.

"I am sent from Pardon to be your contact," Carlos whispered while bending over the horse's leg.

"I expected you tomorrow," Santiago responded, somewhat surprised.

"I am to tell you that the time table has been moved up. Here is the plan," replied Carlos.

"Is it today?" asked Santiago.

"No, tomorrow about mid afternoon, you will take a cartload of rice to the Portuguese ship on the river bank. The cart will not be full as usual due to the fire destroying most of the food. There will be some though. You might want to get the boy to drive it for you. When you get to the ship go up to the crewman standing on the shore and tell him 'I have brought your order'. Say nothing more and nothing less. He will tell you to help him load it. You do as he says. Once on the ship go below with the rice. Look around and try to find something unusual or interesting. Listen to what they say. What ever you do try not to look suspicious. After you have loaded the rice walk up on deck. Find the same crewman and say to him 'the payment should be in the usual way'. Again, nothing more and nothing less," Carlos explained, with a strong serious look in his eyes.

"What if they ask about Diego?" Santiago asked.

"If they do it will be alright to tell them, but keep it short," Carlos stated.

"Yes, I will," Santiago said.

Carlos put the horse's leg down.

"Now about the ship, it is an unusual one, a schooner, with twenty crewmen. That size of a ship really only needs a crew of ten. It has on the deck two life boats. Again that is too many," Carlos explained.

"I wonder why?" Santiago asked.

"I do not know the answer for that. But, I do know that capitán. He is a good sailor and knows how to handle a ship in difficult situations," Carlos replied.

"What about the crewmen?" Santiago asked.

"I only know three of them. Their names are Rollo, Dagger, and Slick. Rollo will be your contact. He is the one with the eye patch.

That fellow Dagger is a dark-skinned libre and got his name because he carries a dagger in his waist band with a diamond in the handle. Claims he will kill anyone who tries to take it. You can also identify him by the two fingers missing from his left hand. In addition, he usually wears a red bandana on his head. Slick wears a white shirt thinks he is good looking to the women. He claims he knows all the women in New Orleans," Carlos explained.

"You have got to be kidding me!" Santiago exclaimed.

"No, Señor, I am serious, and so are they" Carlos said.

"I believe you," Santiago answered.

"These are very dangerous people. They have killed some of our agents in the past. Try not to be the next one. Here is the message that the Coronel wants passed to Rollo," he said, while carefully handing a piece of paper to Santiago.

"I will definitely give that to him," said Santiago, as he quickly hid the note in his pants pocket.

"I will come back and check the filly day after tomorrow," Carlos said loudly as he climbed up onto his wagon.

"Philipe come here," Santiago called out.

"Coming Señor," he said, from the kitchen.

"Tomorrow morning, first thing, go and find a cart to use, preferably Pedro's. If not his then rent one," Santiago ordered.

"Yes, sir. Are we going some where?" Philipe asked.

"No, just going to haul some stuff tomorrow afternoon," Santiago answered.

Chapter 47

The instructions from the farrier Carlos were clear and concise. It should not take long to complete this assignment. After the delivery and making the contact, he and Philipe should be back by supper time.

Philipe had found Pedro's cart at one of the stables. It was being held there by the stable owner, because Pedro had owed him money. Philipe rented it for the day.

The next morning Santiago and Philipe hitched his horse to the cart. After lunch they set out on their assignment.

"I like going places with you and doing the things that you do. I had rather be around the fellas, you know," Philipe said.

"We'll see how you feel about that in say five years from now," replied Santiago with a smile.

After the fire, all of the remaining rice had been placed in one of the warehouses that did not burn. It was guarded by two of the men from the Pardo militia company. As they pulled up in front of the building, a guard stepped forward.

"May I help you Señor?" the guard asked.

"I need six barrels of rice," Santiago answered, while handing him the requisition from the Coronel.

"Very good. Come this way please," the guard said.

As they began picking up the barrels of rice, Santiago noticed three barrels, some what larger, over by the opposite wall.

"What is in those?" Santiago asked.

"That is what is left of all the gun powder after the fire," the guard answered.

"Will we get more soon?" Santiago asked

"I certainly hope so," the guard answered.

"All right, we are ready to head to the ship," Santiago said to Philipe. They climbed up onto the cart and headed toward the edge of the river.

"Which one is it?" Philipe asked, as they pulled up in front of several ships.

"It is the one with the two row boats on the deck," Santiago answered.

After they stopped Santiago said, "You stay with the cart while I go up on deck to find someone."

In no time he came upon Rollo. He recognized him immediately. His appearance was just as Carlos had described him.

"I have brought your rice. Where do you want me to put it?" Santiago asked.

"I will help you and we can stow it below deck," Rollo answered.

"Thanks for the help," Santiago said, as the two men start bringing the barrels onboard.

"Is this all you have?" asked Rollo.

"Yes, most of it was destroyed in the fire. What is left is being rationed," Santiago explained.

"Are you the new contact?" Rollo asked.

"Yes, Diego said if anything happened to him I was to contact you on board this ship. Here is the last message about the militia I was to give to him. Now I give it to you," Santiago explained.

"Were you the one that killed Diego?" Rollo asked, after reading the message.

Santiago was surprised and momentarily caught off guard by this question.

"No!" exclaimed Santiago. "It was Pedro that killed him. He and his two amigos."

"Oh yea, just how do you know that?" Rollo snapped the question with a snarl.

Again, another surprise question. Santiago had to think fast.

"It was easy to find out," Santiago said as he raised his head back in a defiant way.

"How could that be easy, we did not find out," Rollo replied in a gruff voice.

"All right, I tell you," Santiago said. "Yesterday I go to borrow Pedro's cart. I cannot find him. Then I see his cart in front of the stable with a sign on it 'For Sale'. I ask the blacksmith why is he selling Pedro's cart? The man says 'He owes me money and where Pedro is going he will never need a cart again. The Spanish officers have him and the other two. They all three will hang for murder.'"

"Okay, that sounds reasonable," Rollo said, while nodding.

"Now I must go," Santiago said.

"Wait, before you go I want you to meet Dagger and Slick," Rollo said, as the two came walking up.

Just at that time, the ship lurched backwards and began to turn sideways.

"What is happening?" Santiago asked quickly.

Another unexpected event.

"Oh, nothing much. We are going for a little boat ride down the river. Be back around sunrise tomorrow," Rollo said with a large mischievous grin on his face.

"I cannot go with you," Santiago exclaimed as he ran up the stairs and through the hatchway! On deck, he could see that the sun had already gone down. In the twilight he could see Philipe was still sitting on the cart.

"Do not worry, my friend," Dagger said. "We make this run quite often. The capitán knows the river, the currents and the sand bars. So go below and make yourself at home and try some of that rum."

In the dark, he could barely see Philipe disappearing off in the distance. One of the deck hands, was lighting lanterns and hanging them over the side of the ship just about an arm's length above the water. When he finished there was enough light all around the ship to be able to see several yards fore and aft. While they floated with the current two deck hands stood watch aft with an eye out for an errant log.

Philipe watched the ship float down the river all the while wondering what he should do. Further, up on the grassy area behind him he saw an officer on horseback looking out over the river. Philipe ran over to him.

"Sir, the strangest thing just happened," Philipe said breathlessly.

"What is that, young fellow?" questioned the officer.

Philipe explained about Santiago loading barrels of rice and that the ship pulled away with Santiago on board.

"Was the ship supposed to take him somewhere?" the officer asked.

"No, we were going to return to where we live after loading the rice, now I am afraid that something terrible has happened to him," Philipe answered.

"Can you manage the cart by yourself?" the officer asked.

"Yes," replied Philipe.

"Okay, follow me while I go report this to Capitán de la Dolor," the officer said.

Philipe waited outside the headquarters. Soon the capitán came outside and introduced himself.

"Is your name Philipe?" de la Dolor asked.

"Yes, it is," Philipe replied.

"Do you know where the ship is going?" de la Dolor asked.

"No, just that it was going down river," answered Philipe.

"Was your master fighting with any of the crewmen?" de la Dolor asked.

"Not that I could see," answered Philipe.

"What is your master's name?" asked de la Dolor.

"Santiago de Barcelona," Philipe answered.

"Oh, I see," de la Dolor said. "Please wait here while I discuss this with the coronel."

The capitán returned in a few moments.

"Philipe, I have discussed this with Coronel Pardon," de la Dolor said. "He feels that since you saw no foul play and that we do not know what their destination is, then we cannot take any action at this time. On this we both agree."

"Is there anything that can be done tonight?" Philipe asked in a panicky tone.

"No, I am afraid not. If he does not return by tomorrow evening please come and see us again and then we will formulate a plan to search for him," de la Dolor answered.

"Oh, alright," Philipe said, in a dejected tone.

Since it was dark and he had no experience in driving a cart at night, he led the horse and cart up the road as he walked to the boarding house. He felt sad because he feared for Santiago's life.

Meanwhile de la Dolor and Pardon discussed the situation further after Philipe had left.

"This is better than I had hoped for," Pardon said.

"I suspect they may kill Santiago," de la Dolor replied.

"Yes, that could happen," Pardon stated in a sly tone. "Let us not be too quick to rescue our man. You know if he does come back alive, he can tell us where the ship dropped anchor.

"We have been watching them take these evening cruises now for several weeks and we he have never discovered where they go."

"Santiago can answer that question for us when he returns!" de la Dolor exclaimed.

"Correct. We have suspected for quite some time that they have been using that ship to pass information to British agents at some point down river. Now the events of this evening may give us the answer and make it possible to catch them in the act," Pardon said with a crafty smile.

As the ship made its way slowly down the river Santiago was below deck with his three new friends.

"Santiago, we are going up on deck for a smoke. Want to come with us?" Rollo asked.

"Why go up there? Can't you smoke down here?" Santiago asked.

"Capitán's orders. Too much gun powder down here," he answered, pointing to the large barrels in the aft area.

"Okay. I will be up there in a minute, I want to finish tying off these barrels of rice."

Santiago thought '*Why would they need barrels of gun powder, this ship does not have any cannons*'?

As the three went up the ladder, Santiago watched them closely, from below, while pretending to check the barrels. As the last one disappeared through the hatch, he leaned in close to the wall. There was a small space between the boards. On the other side was the capitán's office. He could hear people talking. They were speaking English. The capitán called them by their names, Wilbur Jay and Thomas Fick, as he discussed with them how they are to meet up with some other agents from Bayou Manchac. He quickly committed those names and the conversation to memory. This would be the kind of information Pardon would want to know. As the meeting appeared to be breaking up, he quickly scrambled up the stairs to the deck.

"Hey, mate, what took you so long?" Slick asked.

"Maybe he had a mermaid in one of those barrels," Rollo said laughing.

All four of them leaned against the railing puffing on their pipes and watching the river bank as they went by.

"It looks to me that with all these lanterns you can see a good distance across the water to the shore," Santiago observed.

"Yes," replied Slick. "With the lights we can see the sand bars."

"Then how do you get back to New Orleans?" queried Santiago.

"The current, it takes us down and these row boats take us back up the river," Rollo said.

"I can see you have plenty of men for those boats," Santiago commented.

"This is true," Dagger said.

"Tell the capitán we are turning into Hidden Bayou!" the helmsman yelled, as he strained at turning the wheel.

After entering the bayou, the ship traveled a short distance and then dropped anchor. The crewmen extinguished the lanterns and one of the rowboats was let down over the side. On the aft of the ship, a crewman held up a lighted lantern and slowly swung it back and forth a few times. In a minute, a similar signal could be seen on the edge of the bayou among the trees.

The two men who had been in the capitán's cabin came up on deck and climbed down into the row boat. The rowboat returned to the ship after taking the men to the shore. The second rowboat was lowered into the water and both were attached to the aft of the ship with ropes. Several crewmen were lowered into the boats. Then they began to row out of the bayou. When the ship entered the river, the lanterns were again hung over the sides and on the rowboats as well. It was not long until the ship was moving up river against the current.

After two hours the lights of the city came into view. The landing on the river bank and departing the ship was uneventful. Santiago trudged his way on foot to the boarding house. When he arrived there his last thoughts before he went to sleep were about reporting to the coronel in the morning.

Chapter 48

After lunch, the next day, Santiago walked out of the house by way of the back door passed the kitchen and on toward the barn. Just then, he noticed out of the corner of his left eye, Carlos the farrier, pulling up to the side of the street by the house. Given the events of the preceding day, he expected Carlos to come to see him earlier.

"Carlos I'm over here by the barn," he yelled, as he noticed him walking toward the front of the house.

"Oh, there you are," Carlos replied.

"I'm glad to see you have come back to check on the mare," Santiago replied, in a very loud voice so that anyone close by would be sure to hear. The two of them walked together into the barn and stood by the horse.

"Did you make it back here last night in good order?" Carlos asked.

"Yes, I tell you it was ingenious the way those fellas maneuvered that ship," Santiago said, with half a smile.

"You are correct," Carlos replied while looking at the horse's hind leg. "I think it very wise not to under estimate them."

"I agree."

"About how far down river did you go?" inquired Carlos.

"I would say about four leagues."

"Could you make out any landmarks?"

"Not really, it was very dark by that time and all the shore line looked the same. Oh yes, there was one thing, the helmsman called out to the capitán that they were approaching 'Hidden Bayou'," Santiago said.

"That is good. I think we know where that place is located," stated Carlos.

"There is something else," Santiago said. "That capitán met with two men before we got to the bayou. Their names were Wilbur Jay and Thomas Fick."

"I do not think I know those names," Carlos said, while checking out side the barn door to see if anyone was near.

"He gave them instructions on how to handle messages to and from Bayou Manchac," Santiago said.

"Do you think you would be able to recognize them again?" asked Carlos.

"Possibly, but I did not get that good of a look at them. Immediately after the meeting they left the ship," Santiago answered.

"That is some very useful information and I will be sure to record it in the dossier. Before I was an officer I was a scribe, so writing things down is very easy for me," Carlos added.

"I can see that would be very helpful in your profession," Santiago said.

"The coronel wants you to go back to the ship later today, before supper, and make arrangements to have some future meetings with Rollo at a local tavern such as Olivier's or Derneville's," Carlos stated.

"I can do that today. Now that they know me, it should be easy to go on board that ship," Santiago agreed.

"Be careful, my friend do not let your guard down," Carlos said, as he and Santiago left the barn. "I will be back tomorrow afternoon at this same time to check the other leg."

"Philipe have my horse saddled and ready in about an hour," Santiago yelled toward the house.

"Where are we going?" Philipe asked leaning out the second story window.

"We are not going anywhere. I have to go tend to some business before supper. Which reminds me, what are we having for supper?" Santiago asked.

"Crawfish and rice," Philipe answered, as he came out of the back door.

As Santiago approached the ship he found it to be in the exact same spot as the last time he was there.

"Hello, Rollo," he yelled as he walked up the plank.

"Santiago, is that you?" Rollo asked while he yelled from the deck.

"Yes, may I come aboard?" Santiago asked.

"Yes, of course, my friend," Rollo agreed.

"I have some interesting information we need to talk about in a nice quiet place. Maybe Olivier's?" Santiago asked.

"Yes, I know the place. As a matter of fact I have been there several times," Rollo replied. "How about tomorrow evening?"

"That will be perfect, see you then," Santiago said, as he waved and turned to walk back down the plank.

As he got up on his saddle, he saw an officer on horse-back further down the waters edge. He could not tell who it was, but the man was definitely watching that ship. He felt safer knowing that one of the officers was keeping an eye on him. Pardon is keeping his promise.

The next evening arrived quickly and Santiago wondered where the time had gone. He left his horse at the hitching post in front of the tavern. This time with his less expensive saddle on it.

"Hello, my friend," said Rollo. "I am glad to see you could make it tonight."

"Oh good, you have gotten us a table away from the door," Santiago answered.

"Yes, away from prying eyes and all those flies," Rollo replied.

"What are you drinking?" asked Santiago.

"Madeira," answered Rollo.

"Oh, Roseta a glass of the Madeira please," Santiago asked.

He felt that now there was a bond of friendship between him and Rollo and because of this, he felt more relaxed now in his presence.

"Tell me what is the information that you have for me?" Rollo asked in a hushed tone.

"I found…," Santiago started to answer, but stopped as Roseta approached the table with his drink.

"Here is your drink, Santiago and I am glad to see you back in here again," Roseta said, with her usual big smile.

"Thank you very much," Santiago replied, as she turned and walked away.

"Now, as I was saying, I found out that during the fire the warehouse containing all the regiment's fire arms was completely burned to the ground along with all of the muskets," Santiago stated with a serious look.

"I would say that misfortune would leave them at a very great disadvantage," Rollo said.

"At this point they have not received any shipments of replacements," whispered Santiago.

"Makes for an interesting turn of events for them."

"Where you here during the fire?" Santiago inquired, as he sipped his wine.

"On that ship of course. Seemed like to me the safest place," Rollo stated.

"You fared better than I did. I was on the north side of the city," Santiago added.

"How did you keep from getting burned?" Rollo asked.

"Simple, I jumped onto my horse and ran away," Santiago answered.

"Just like everybody else. By the way, I wonder what are the chances of getting Diego's money from those officers? I figure he had maybe three hundred pesos," Rollo inquired.

"I do not know," answered Santiago. "I suppose I can ask around."

"You could say you were a friend of his and that he owed you money," suggested Rollo.

"That is not a bad idea and it just might work. Now that you mentioned money, I am a little short. How about you give me my salary?" asked Santiago.

"That's a fair question now that Diego is dead. I will take it up with the ship capitán."

"All of my clothes were destroyed in the fire. It would be nice to have more than one pair of pants," replied Santiago.

"My friend, we will not let you go around naked!" Rollo yelled, with a laugh.

Chapter 49

The next morning Santiago went downstairs for an early breakfast. He was the only one up, beside one of the housekeepers, who was fixing the breakfast. The food was not ready yet, but he was glad to see the coffee was.

"I will just have a cup now and come back to eat later," he said.

"You are welcome, sir," she said, while she wiped the sweat off of her forehead.

"Is it this hot i
n here every morning?" he asked her with a smile.

"Oh yes, sir," she answered.

"I must tell you that the food here is very good," he said, as he stepped out of the door heading for the barn.

After saddling his horse he started out early to Pardon's office, in an attempt to catch him before the day got busy. He was in luck, Pardon arrived at the same time.

"Oh good morning, Santiago," Pardon said.

"Same to you, sir," Santiago replied. "I hoped I would catch you early before things became busy."

"You did just that," Pardon answered. "Has something special come up?"

"I was hoping to get started on the next meeting with Rollo," he answered, as they both stepped into the office.

Just then, the guard arrived to begin his shift outside the door.

"See that we are not disturbed," Pardon ordered.

Pardon lit the table top lanterns as both sat on opposite sides of the makeshift desk.

"Let's see now," Pardon said, looking at some of the papers on the desk. "Oh yes, here we are, tonight at Olivier's, see if you can get there a little earlier than Rollo. That way the man I will have shadowing you will be able to get a centrally located table before Rollo arrives."

"That should be no trouble," Santiago answered.

"Tonight I want you to tell him that the scheduled shipment of gun powder, for Mobile, will be withheld indefinitely," Pardon stated.

"I see no problem doing that," Santiago answered.

"Also see if you can strike up a conversation about the fire. Then verify where he and his two shipmates were at that time" Pardon requested.

After saying that Pardon noticed Santiago was staring off toward the door and did not respond. He appeared to be preoccupied by some other thoughts.

"Santiago, are you okay?" Pardon asked.

"I am sorry, sir, may I discuss something with you? A personal problem that is somewhat off the subject." Santiago asked.

"Why yes, of course," Pardon responded slowly, with a skeptical look on his face. "Please tell me what it is."

"For the last few days I have been plagued with guilt feelings. At first, I did not understand why. Then it came to me that down inside I had those feelings because I had betrayed my homeland. The more I thought about it that way the clearer the realization became. You can see, I'm sure, that saying this puts me in an awkward position," Santiago stated.

"What do you think we should do about it?" Pardon asked, in a frustrated tone.

"Basically, I feel as though I have betrayed my country," he said, groping for the words. "I do not want to be a double agent any longer. I would like to be a spy just for Spain only. However, I realize I have an obligation to you as well. Is there any way to redeem myself for what I have done since arriving here?" Santiago asked, in a pleading voice.

"I'm sure you realize that we have several activities planned against the British which involve your knowledge of the situation," Pardon stated loudly.

"Yes, of course I do realize that," Santiago replied.

"I cannot promise you anything. The only thing I can do is to talk this over with Pound. He is the person who has the authority to make such a change. In the meantime we will continue on as planned," Pardon replied sharply.

"Yes, of course..." Santiago said, while being interrupted by the guard knocking on the door.

Pardon stood up, walked to the door and opened it. There on the other side was the guard and a tall man in a uniform. The uniform was not familiar to Santiago. The coronel and the guard exchanged a few words and Pardon came back to where Santiago was sitting.

"You must excuse this interruption, but I have a visitor who insists on seeing me now. I tell you this, why don't you stay outside with the guard and I will finish our meeting with you after he leaves," Pardon said.

"Of course coronel," Santiago said, quickly leaving the room. As he passed the naval officer, he vaguely remembered where he had seen that uniform before. Outside the door, he stood beside the guard.

"That is the Portuguese Naval Attaché," the guard said.

"Portugal is still an ally of Spain, are they not?" Santiago asked the guard.

"Yes," the guard replied.

That confirmed what Santiago had remembered about the uniform. He paced back and forth in front of the door not getting too far away. The closer he was the better he could hear what they were saying.

The Attaché described how he was sent here by his government to observe the military installations around the city, especially of the harbor. The man spoke fluent Portuguese. Santiago recognized it from the time he lived in Barcelona. Seeing Portuguese people there was not unusual. As their conversation, about defensive gun emplacements, began to wain, it became louder and seemed like they were getting closer to the door. It was at that point he heard the naval officer say something, in Portuguese, that was very unusual, but very familiar.

"That, my friend maybe a difficult place to put a cannon, especially with all those damned mosquitos," Pardon said.

"Yes, of course, there is always the unexpected you know," the Naval Attaché answered, in Portuguese.

Santiago stopped dead in his tracks. He did not move. He could not move. He could not believe what he just heard. He said to himself *This is more than just a coincidence.* There must be some connection between this fellow and that Major Pullman in London. He thought to himself *I must come up with a way to break this fellow's cover and flush him out.*

As the attaché came out of the office Santiago was standing just beyond the door way. Santiago stepped forward and introduced himself speaking in Catalan. The attaché likewise introduced himself speaking in perfect Portuguese.

Then as the attaché began to walk away Santiago said in perfect English.

"Very nice to come upon you this way, ol' chap."

Very quickly, the attaché responded, "Yes, of course, right oh....", in perfect English.

The attaché stopped immediately. He turned his head only so slightly left towards Santiago and cut his eyes towards him for a second or two. Then he quickly walked off from the warehouse and turned to the right toward the Portuguese ship on the shore.

Santiago ran after him for a few steps to see which way he went. Then he turned back and went into the coronel's office. He explained the whole thing to the coronel breathlessly.

"Are you absolutely sure?" Pardon asked.

"There is no doubt what I heard and he knows that I know and he saw me here. He is making a run for it," Santiago explained.

"I think the best thing for you to do now is to remain here while I assemble the militia," Pardon said to Santiago, almost breathlessly.

"Go and find Pound immediately," Pardon yelled to the guard. "Wherever he is and whatever he's doing, get him and bring him here. It is urgent."

With musket in hand, the guard took off for another building close to the warehouse.

Pardon ordered another guard to find Capitán de la Dolor. When he arrived, orders were given to him to assemble the Pardo Militia Company for a military action, possibly overnight.

About one-half hour later, de la Dolor arrived. At that same time the corporal assigned to watch the Portuguese ship came to Pardon's office.

"Yes, what is it?" de la Dolor asked the corporal.

"Sir, the Portuguese ship has weighed anchor and is headed down river," he said.

"Thank you. Return to your post," de la Dolor ordered.

"Capitán, you will take your company by ship down river to the area of Hidden Bayou," Pardon ordered. "You will drop anchor one quarter league this side of that Bayou. Take your company by land, from there south to the Bayou, intercept and capture everyone on board that ship and in the immediate area. If they refuse, take them by force.

"Also, you will take Santiago with you. I am pressing him into service in this regiment as a second lieutenant under your command.

Since he has already made this trip to Hidden Bayou, he will be of great value to you during this mission. Do either of you have any questions?" Pardon asked.

"No sir," they both answered.

"Santiago draw what supplies you need from the quartermaster. Good luck gentlemen," Pardon said.

"Yes, sir," de la Dolor answered quickly. He and Santiago left the office.

Just then, there was a knock on the door. It was Pound and he let himself in.

"I came over as quick as I could," he said.

"We have had a bit of excitement here in the last couple of hours," Pardon explained.

"I noticed the Pardo Militia Company getting ready for some kind of action," Pound replied.

"Here in a nutshell is the story: Santiago was here for a meeting about plans for his activities. During that time, a Portuguese Naval Attaché came by to see me. I had Santiago stand outside for a moment. Afterwards Santiago saw through his disguise and managed to flush him out!"

"My God are you serious?"

"That attaché, or whatever he really is, took off like his pants were on fire."

"Had Santiago ever seen him before?"

"He indicated that he had not," Pardon replied. "Just something about his speech that gave him away."

"Why that is an excellent piece of undercover work on Santiago's part!" Pound exclaimed.

"This attaché fellow boarded the Portuguese ship and the whole bunch took off down river. I've sent de la Dolor and his company after them with orders to bring them back dead or alive," Pardon stated, as he leaned back in his chair.

"That is a very good plan. I will back you all the way on that," Pound stated.

"Now that brings me around to something Santiago said before the attaché fiasco started. He has guilt feelings about being a spy for the British. He says he had rather work only for Spain, which is of course his homeland. I told him we would talk and think it over," Pardon explained.

"I think that is also a good plan. Let us see how this action down river goes and then we should talk some more about Santiago," Pound stated, just before he left.

Chapter 50

Whicle the schooner, with about fifty militiamen and officers, slowly made its way down river, Santiago could see that the sun was low in the sky and it would soon be dark.

About an hour later they dropped anchor at a cleared area along the shore. It was about one-quarter league north of Hidden Bayou and was a perfect place to off-load men and supplies.

When all the men were in the woods they fanned out in a single line from east to west and facing south. With guns ready and bayonets fixed. The bright moon light on that clear night gave just enough glow to see several feet ahead. They all walked quietly and carefully, avoiding twigs and dried leaves as much as possible.

After one-half hour they spotted the light from a campfire ahead about one-hundred paces. The capitán divided the men into two groups. He took one group and Santiago the other. Their plan was to approach the camp from an angle on each side. The British, numbering about twenty, would have the bayou to the backs. This approach would cut off any escape.

The militia observed them for a few minutes. Half of the British were sitting around a campfire eating while the rest were packing up equipment. There were three horses twenty paces to the left of the campfire.

Santiago recognized one of them at the campfire as the phony attaché. He stood out because he was taller than the rest.

The capitán quietly ordered both groups to each form two rows facing the enemy. The first row was kneeling. When all the men were in positon, fifty paces from the campfire he yelled.

"THIS IS CAPITÁN de la DOLOR OF THE LOUISIANA REGIMENT. STAND UP, PUT YOUR HANDS IN THE AIR AND DO NOT MOVE."

Some of the British were startled while others ran for their gun rack. None of them obeyed the capitán's command.

The capitán gave the order, "Fire."

This was followed by a loud report from multiple muskets firing all along the militia line.

Several of the Brits at the campfire fell over backwards. Others broke for the boat in the bayou. All of the horses scattered, one running along in front of Santiago toward the trees.

One Brit picked up what looked to be a small cannon and began to aim it at the capitán. Santiago pulled his pistol and took aim at him. Before he could fire one of the militia shot the fellow. Just then Santiago saw the phony attaché on the right running toward the trees where the horse had gone. Santiago moved quickly to intercept him.

The phony attaché stopped and looked around for the horse. He did not see Santiago. Santiago stepped out from behind a tree while he raised his pistol to aim. At that point the phony attaché saw him.

"So it is you," the phony attaché said in perfect English, as he pulled out his pistol, cocked it and aimed at Santiago.

When Santiago had his pistol leveled at the phony attaché he realized he had not cocked it. In the one second it took Santiago to cock the hammer back was enough time for the other man to get off a shot. The slug struck Santiago in the left arm just below the shoulder causing a flesh wound.

While the phony attaché was reloading Santiago fired. The round hit the man in the forehead knocking him over backwards. The phony attaché lay motionless in the grass. Santiago approached and could see the right side of his face covered in blood.

By this time the battle was over and Santiago went to find the capitán and report what had happened.

After hearing the explanation the capitán said, "Let us go and look at this fellow. Maybe I can recognize him."

When they arrived at the spot the body was no where to be found. However, his pistol and some blood were on the ground.

Santiago asked the capitán, "Do you suppose he could have gotten away on that horse?"

"It is possible," the capitán answered. "We will question the prisoners to find if one of them knows."

They found one prisoner who did see a man on a horse riding to the north just as the gunfire stopped.

"The man who escaped is on horseback riding at full speed and is probably one league away from here by know. We are on foot and would never be able to catch him. Now we must take the prisoners and captured equipment back to New Orleans," the capitán explained to Santiago.

"Now we know where he is headed and the coronel can send out the militia to search for him," Santiago replied.

"Get the men ready to move out," the capitán ordered.

"Yes sir," Santiago answered. "But what about the British ship in the bayou?"

"We are going to leave five men here to guard it and the two remaining horses. The ship is a war prize and will be taken to Havana to be refitted for our navy," the capitán answered.

The return to New Orleans was slow and uneventful, arriving shortly after sunup the next day.

When Santiago entered the coronel's office after lunch, he immediately noticed that Jerome Pound was already there.

"Please come in and have a seat," said Pardon, with a smile.

"You did a very good piece of work flushing out that phony naval attaché. Your work with the capitán at Hidden Bayou was very heroic and well done. By the way how is that flesh wound?" Pound asked.

"Thank you, sir. It is healing nicely," he answered.

"Before you arrived we have been putting together a report on the military activities of yesterday and last night. What I am about to give you is a summary of that report.

"After you identified the attaché, he immediately made his way to the Portuguese ship. At that time, he obviously warned the crew of the situation. They in turn weighed anchor and headed down river for their rendezvous point in Hidden Bayou. We believe that they would meet up with their people from Bayou Manchac, abandon the ship and head north on foot back to that place. From there they would make a further escape," Pardon explained.

"Sounds like they had an escape plan in place ahead of time, don't you think," Santiago interjected.

"Yes, we agree with that," Pardon stated.

"Now to continue, Mr. Pound and I felt it was absolutely necessary to stop them at any cost. So to that end, we assembled a company of the Pardo Militia, commanded by Capitán de la Dolor and yourself as a lieutenant, to pursue and intercept them. Those British agents were to be brought back here dead or alive. You and the militia caught up with them just after they disembarked from the ship.

"They refused to surrender and a skirmish commenced. The Brits were taken by complete surprise. Most of them were killed. The phony attaché escaped, but we will be searching for him. The prisoners, that survived, will soon be on their way to Havana for trial," Pardon said.

"We had suspected that Portuguese ship for a long time. However, we never had enough evidence to arrest any of those fellows. It was your quick action with that attaché that put the icing on the cake, so to speak. If it had not been for you we may never have been able to dispatch this whole bunch," Pound complimented Santiago.

"Now at this point I think we can close the book on this spy episode," Pardon stated. "As a matter of fact, by my estimation, the end result of this action has been to completely remove all of the British spies from this city. Santiago that is something you can be very proud of."

"Oh one other thing," began Pound. "I think we should reward each of the men in that militia company. Say, fifteen silver pesos?"

"I think that is an excellent idea," agreed Pardon.

"Very good then," Pound replied. "I must go now or else I will be late for a meeting with Governor Miro."

After he left the room, Santiago stayed behind so he could discuss his future with the coronel.

"Santiago, Mr. Pound has already stated how he feels about your performance, and I would like to add to that my sentiments as well."

"Yes, sir, of course," he responded with a smile.

"The aspect I like most about your work is the way you think the same as we do. That is a very important requirement in this business. Before you arrived today, he and I discussed at length about your future role here. I brought up the fact that you have demonstrated an allegiance to Spain. Obviously a very necessary quality. The fact that you have shown these excellent traits, primarily on your own, allows us to look on your future here with us in great favor. We have a great need for someone with your talents for a special project we have in mind," Pardon explained.

"Will I have to continue on as a double agent?" Santiago asked.

"It just so happens that Mr. Pound and I were discussing the overall effects of your actions in exposing that phony attaché. As I said before, by our calculation this episode did away with all of the British spies here in New Orleans. Therefore, the need for you to work as a double agent no longer exists. In short, we have decided to grant your request to work only for us."

"I am very happy to hear that," Santiago stated.

"Yes, I thought you might be," Pardon replied. "Your new status begins now."

"That sounds even better," Santiago said, with a very wide smile.

"It is drawing near to evening now and I think we should continue this discussion first thing in the morning," Pardon stated.

"I agree," Santiago said.

As he walked back to his boarding house he thought about what he had done in the last two days. He was proud of himself and of his Catalonian heritage.

Chapter 51

The next morning could not come fast enough for Santiago. He was awake before the first rooster crowed. Dressed and down to breakfast before all the kitchen ladies were up. He passed the time by getting his horse fed and watered.

While eating with Maria Pauley and Philipe, he could hardly hold back his desire to tell them about his happiness. However, his better judgment told him he should wait until a time when all the details of his position had been presented to him.

By the time he finished eating he noticed that the sun was already above the horizon. It was time for him to go.

"I have something for you that I think you will like," Pardon said.

"Oh what is that?" Santiago asked *thinking what else could they possibly give me.*

"It is a financial reward for your activities over the last few weeks. I'm sure you recall the money that was confiscated when Diego was killed. It does not belong to Spain, the owner is dead and no relatives or heirs have come forward. Therefore, we think you should have it," Pardon explained, as he took the leather bag out of his saddle bags.

"That is very gracious of you, sir," Santiago said.

"I think you will find in there three hundred fifty silver pesos," replied Pardon.

"I trust you, sir," said Santiago.

"Now, as for your official status with us. You will have the position of a consultant to us for military affairs. Also the salary of a capitán in the Louisiana Regiment and you will report only to me. All information you develop during any investigation will be strictly confidential and be discussed only with me. Agreed?" asked Pardon.

"Agreed," answered Santiago.

"You will have authority to view all documents in this Colony regardless of their location," stated Pardon.

"Does that include even the governor's correspondence?" asked Santiago.

"Yes, if you encounter any difficulties just let me know and I will take care of it," Pardon said.

"Very good, sir," replied Santiago.

"The reason for this special assignment is that there are several of us in the military who are very suspicious about how the recent fire began. This is a good time for us to discuss the matter," Pardon said.

"Yes, sir," Santiago replied.

"You will conduct a preliminary investigation. Now let us start with the facts that we know so far. Keep in mind some of these so called facts may sound more like rumors than fact:

"First, the fire is said to have started in the home of Vicente Nunez, the treasurer. It was the Good Friday before Easter Sunday. That was a recognized holiday for all the citizens, both military and civilian. See if you can find anyone who was on the street and witnessed the fire begin.

"Second, it started in the afternoon about one-half hour after one o'clock. Because of the holiday the streets were deserted and all shops and businesses were closed.

"Third, there is this rumor going around to the effect that after the fire started an unknown priest stood in the doorway of the church and would not let anyone in to ring the bell to warn the town's people of the emergency. Some thing about he did not want the bell rung on Good Friday," Pardon explained.

"That sounds interesting," said Santiago.

"Fourth, even I personally have heard that the fire began almost simultaneously in several parts of the city. I'm not quite sure how that would happen?" said Pardon.

"That does sound somewhat suspicious," added Santiago.

"Fifth, someone has said, almost immediately, before all the embers had extinguished, that the total loss will be somewhere between six and seven million pesos. They did not have time to get estimates of damages from property owners, so how could they know this value so quickly?" inquired Pardon.

"I will check on that also," Santiago said.

"Oh one more thing," began Pardon. "see if you can pinpoint where those crewmen from the Portuguese ship were at the time the fire began."

"Okay, looks like I have plenty to start with," Santiago responded.

"Remember, for reasons of secrecy, there will be no written documents retained by us concerning this matter," Pardon reminded him.

"Yes, sir, I will definitely keep that in mind," Santiago assured him.

"We will meet back here in one week to discuss your progress," Pardon commanded.

Santiago left the office and headed back to the boarding house. He needed to find people to talk to about all the subjects he had been given to investigate. Who in the city would have that kind of information? The notaries, the ones in the community who record contracts, and the like, would probably have talked to some people who witnessed the fire.

Then there would be the people in the government such as the governor and his assistants. The priests would talk to their parishioners and by doing so, they would hear reports about the fire. And then there would be the coronel's own officers in his regiment. They would have helped rescue people.

By his calculation he had many people to talk to who would have seen and experienced the fire from many of its' different points of view. He calculated that to get answers to most of the questions would take at least a week or maybe more.

About eight days later when Santiago felt he had enough information he returned to Pardon's office. It was a good thing that this meeting was starting in the morning, for he had many things to tell the coronel.

"Tell me what you have found out?" Pardon asked.

"Since I started on this investigation I have been back and forth from one end of this city to the other several times. I talked to many people. Some were not so willing to talk, because they did not know me. When I mentioned that I worked for you and Mr. Pound, then everyone was willing to sit down with me."

"I thought using our names might be helpful for you," Pardon said, with a quaint smile.

"Your names were very influential in opening doors and loosening tongues."

"So, tell me what did you find out about where the fire started?" asked Pardon.

"I could not find anyone who saw the fire in it's initial stage of burning. However, that did not surprise me due to the holiday. Everyone would be staying at home and not on the streets. Plus that time of day is the customary time for siesta," Santiago answered.

"Alright that sounds reasonable, so what about the priest in the doorway of the church?" Pardon asked.

"For that one I had a conversation with my cousin Tomas. He said he was not aware of anyone, priest or otherwise, that stood in the doorway and stopped people from coming into the church. He and I both walked from what was left of the church to the place where the fire supposedly started. A distance between those two is somewhere on the order of only one-half to one block? If the fire was as voracious and fast moving as everyone has said, then it seems to me that within one-half hour the church would have been on fire. I really doubt that anyone stood in the doorway of the church while it was burning down," Santiago explained.

"Then, what you are saying is that the church was one of the first buildings to burn down?" asked Pardon.

"Yes, the strong wind, out of the south, at that time also helped push the fire toward the church."

"Now, how about this map that your friend Diego came up with? You know the one, drawn by a Captain Pittman of the British Army back in 1770."

"Oh yes, of course that one," Santiago began. "That is the one he got from who knows where. I found it interesting because it was definitely a military map. I think it reveals the British interest in our defensive positions. Information to be used by them to plan an attack on this city," Santiago explained.

"You certainly have found some intriguing answers," Pardon said.

"There is still more that I have to work on," stated Santiago.

"Such as?" Pardon asked.

"For one, I want to talk more with the two Notaries, Pedesclaux and Perdomo," Santiago explained.

"Please by all means do that," Pardon agreed.

"Give me a few more days," Santiago requested.

"Yes, return when you have more information," Pardon said.

Santiago returned three days later.

"I spoke with Pedesclaux and asked him if he had many people come to him and ask about filing claims. He said only a few. Then I asked him if he heard any rumor about the fire starting in Nunez's house. He said he had not seen any document from Nunez stating that. He also said that Governor Miro had given the citizens, who had damages eight days to file a written claim with the government. He also said neither he nor Perdomo had any damages from the fire."

"What does all that mean to us?" Pardon asked.

"I believe that it is another piece of evidence that the origin of the fire is unclear," Santiago answered.

"Okay, what else?" Pardon asked.

"There are also rumors going around that there were numerous explosions during the fire. I can attest to that myself."

"But, there is nothing conclusive?" Pardon asked with a frown.

"No," replied Santiago.

"Were you able to find out where the crewmen of that Portuguese ship were at the time the fire started?"

"Again no," Santiago answered.

"Let us do this," Pardon suggested. "Let us now look at all the possible suspects who would have a motive."

"Okay then there would be, first of all, the group in Bayou Manchac," Santiago pointed out eagerly.

"How so?" asked Pardon.

"One way to increase their trading business on the river would be to destroy this city."

"I agree," Pardon began explaining. "However, I do not think those folks would have enough manpower or guns to follow through. So that would eliminate them."

"Secondly, there would be the slaves who have been revolting in the Caribbean Islands," Santiago suggested.

"Possibly, but I think they would be at the same disadvantages as those people up the river in Bayou Manchac. Few guns and even fewer people. This would eliminate them also," Pardon answered.

"Okay thirdly, the other day I heard one of your officers talking about some fellow from America named Wilkinson," Santiago said.

"You must mean the General James Wilkinson."

"Yes, that is him," Santiago began. "It was said that he has a scheme to get the territories of Tennessee and Kentucky away from the

Americans and have them join the Louisiana Colony. He says he can provide a small army to help with that. However, I think that he is a threat to the American's and not any threat at all to the Louisiana Colony."

"I think you are right about that fellow," stated Pardon.

"That leaves only one other candidate, the British," replied Santiago.

"Now there is a group of people with a serious motive, opportunity and certainly the tools to get the job done," Pardon suggested.

"Galvez pushed the English out of the Florida West Parishes and took Mobile and Pensacola away from them. Now they want it back and in a big way, with an eye on New Orleans," Santiago said.

"If they were the ones who set the fire then they made a serious miscalculation in their planning. What do you think?" Pardon asked.

"If I were a betting man I would put my money on the British," Santiago answered.

"That pretty much wraps up this whole investigation then," concluded Pardon.

"Now then, I was wondering about my freedom?" Santiago asked. "I think I have done a good job, do you agree?"

"Actually Pound and I have already discussed this matter and have decided that with the outstanding performance of your duties that you are free to go. All the charges against you have been dissolved. Good luck, my friend."

"Thank you sir," Santiago said, as he walked out the door.

Chapter 52

Santiago mounted his horse, an animal he was very proud to be seen on, and slowly made his way to the boarding house. Occasionally he would stop and raise himself up in the saddle, and turn to look out over the city of tents. Looking over the piles of burned wood, he could see the river and remembered, with a feeling of melancholy, all that had happened over the last few weeks.

As he arrived at the rear of the house, he realized his time here had come to an end. He must explain to everyone at the house what he felt he had to do. Just then, he heard a voice behind him. Without turning to see who it was, he knew.

"Señor, Señor, you have been gone so long today. Where have you been?" asked Philipe, as he walked up to him. Pants legs rolled up one longer than the other and a hat turned side ways.

"Come inside with me and I will tell you all about it," Santiago said.

"You really will, you promise?" asked Philipe.

"While I put my horse up you go tell everybody to gather around the table, I want to talk to them," Santiago ordered.

"I know all of you have had questions about what I have been involved with ever since I arrived here," Santiago said.

He explained for more than an hour about how he came to be here and what he had done. Describing all of the masquerade of being a man looking for a plantation and having plenty of family money, and the association with Diego. The time he was arrested for Diego's murder. And finally, what he had done for Pardon and how it led to his freedom.

"I have made up my mind that the best thing for my future is to return to Barcelona and reconnect with my family," Santiago said, with a sad tone.

"How long will you stay before you leave?" Philipe asked, in a quite tone.

"I think a month. It will take me that long to make arrangements," Santiago answered.

Maria Pauley sat there quietly crying and Juliana immediately jumped up and quickly walked out of the house to the kitchen. He could feel the great tension in the air.

"Philipe, come with me and let us go for a walk," Santiago said.

"Oh no, I want to stay here!" he exclaimed in a defiant voice.

"Come on, the walk will do you good," Santiago ordered.

"Alright," Philipe said, as he stood up slowly.

They took their time and walked on the street toward Burns's horse pasture.

"They are both in love with you. Don't you know?" Philipe asked.

"Who is they?" Santiago asked almost indignantly.

"Widow Pauley and Juliana of course," he said.

"I'm sure you are mistaken. Those two women are very pretty and they will have no trouble finding a man after I have gone," Santiago explained, with a fatherly voice.

"Will you take me with you?" Philipe asked, in an excited begging voice.

"I wish you could go with me," Santiago said, while he put his arm around Philipe's shoulders. "But, you see I do not know what awaits me when I get there. I have not had any contact with my family there for several years. I do not know if any of them are still alive."

"I'm a big guy and I can take care of myself, here or anywhere," Philipe responded, almost yelling.

"I'm sorry, but I think that you can very well take care of yourself now. The best thing for your future is to stay here with the widow. She likes you very much you know," Santiago said with a smile.

They made their way back to the house and it was almost time for supper.

The next morning Santiago went to search for his cousin Tomas. He found him in the mercado buying vegetables. He explained to him all of the same things that he spoke about to Philipe and the others at the house. As they walked for a short distance, they talked. Tomas talked about Santiago's future. Then he told him what he knew about the family in Catalonia.

"My son," he began. "You have changed a great deal in the short time you have been here. I think now you have a stronger moral heading and it will serve you well."

They talked a little longer then embraced and said their good byes.

That afternoon Santiago took his horse and saddle to one of the livery stables. He and the owner made arrangements to find a buyer for them.

On his way home, he walked by the river's edge. There many ships were at anchor. He looked for one that would be bound for Cadiz, Spain. He noticed a ship that looked vaguely familiar. As he walked closer, he found two men standing by the gangplank. He asked them.

"Is this one going to Cadiz?"

"Yes, but we just arrived here yesterday. It will probably be three weeks before we leave," one of the men answered.

"That will be great and it will give me just the right amount of time to take care of all my affairs."

"Would you like to book passage now?" he asked.

"Sure. Are you the capitán?" Santiago asked.

"No, I am the owner. The capitán is not here now. He should be back sometime later. Did you want to talk to him?"

"Not now, but maybe later. What is the name of the ship?"

"It is the *Adriana,*" the man said.

"Really!" exclaimed Santiago. "What is the Capitán's name?"

"Smith," the man replied.

"Oh, how much?" Santiago asked in a quiet tone.

"Fifty pesos for a stateroom," the man answered.

"I'll take it," Santiago said, as he counted out the coins.

On his way back to the house he began to feel like his plan for leaving was coming together.

The next three weeks passed very slowly and the days were filled with talking to Philipe and the others and thinking about what may lie ahead in Barcelona.

Finally, the day of departure arrived and he loaded all he had into a small trunk. He placed it on the cart and hitched up the mare. He had already sold his horse and saddle and decided to keep his knife and gun. After saying goodbye to everyone, he boarded the ship.

It was just after lunch, when the ship slowly pulled away from the shore and headed down river. He stayed on deck and watched Philipe, Maria Pauley and Juliana as he drifted away.

They made it passed the Baliza and then into the gulf. In a few hours, it would be dark. The ship was now surrounded on all sides by the ocean. His thoughts were more on the voyage ahead than on the friends he left behind.

He heard a voice behind from one of the crewmen.

"Okay, mates, now turn her into the wind," the voice said.

That voice sounded vaguely familiar. He turned around to see who it was and all he could see was a man's back. Then he saw the blond colored hair in the back laying out from under a first mate's hat.

Then he thought of who it might be, but that's not possible. Just maybe. So he walked up behind the man.

"A cockroach for your supper man," Santiago said.

The first mate turned around and looked at him.

"What the bloody....," he started to say, but stopped abruptly.

"SANTIAGO, what in the bloody h. are you doing here?" Joseph asked, with a giant grin as he put his arms around him.

"Joseph, you are the last person I expected to see on this ship."

"Same here, mate," Joseph said, still grinning. "Why don't we get together after supper tonight? I'll be off then and we can share some rum and catch up on old times."

"Sounds great and that will give me time to unpack," Santiago answered.

"Have you been below deck yet near the galley?" Joseph asked.

"No, why do you ask that? Is the food really good?" Santiago asked.

"Oh yea, man, there is something really good down there. See you later," Joseph said, as he and another crewman walked to the stern.

Santiago was not quite sure what Joseph meant, but it was probably that they had a good cook. Something like that can make a sea voyage more enjoyable.

As he walked through the passage way below deck near the galley the smell of good cooked food filled the air. As he started to enter his stateroom he saw someone out of the corner of his eye walk out of the galley and into the passage way. From a distance, he could not see who it was so he walked closer. It was a woman he could tell for sure and she looked familiar. She was carrying a tray of food and dishes. She suddenly turned and entered the captain's dining area.

He thought that in just a moment she would come out so he waited by the door.

As she came out of the door, she was looking back at the table and did not see Santiago. She ran into him and then looked up at him. It was Maria, the cook from Newgate Prison in London.

Her eyes were as big as could be.

"Santiago! I am speechless," she began saying. "Where did you come from? Why are you on this ship? I must be dreaming."

"No you are not dreaming, it is really me and I am on my way to Cadiz," Santiago said.

"I am contracted to be the cook on this ship until we get back into Liverpool, which will be after Cadiz, you know."

"Yes, I know. I see you are busy now so we should talk some more when you are off duty," Santiago said.

"I would like that very much," she answered.

"I can see this is going to be a very wonderful voyage," he said, while holding her in his arms.

AFTERWARD

More than one hundred documents, left behind by the survivors, were reviewed before the preparation of this manuscript. Those were only a portion of the total. Many more remain to be discovered, insuring the future return of Santiago.